More praise for Amanda Cross and *The Puzzled Heart*

"Part of the art of being a successful mystery writer is the ability to create a leading character who remains as compelling in the twentieth outing as he or she was in the first. Moreover, a new reader should be able to pick up any book in a series and get enough information about the sleuth to be able to follow the plot without saying, 'Huh?' Amanda Cross does this brilliantly in *The Puzzled Heart*. . . . What makes this book a delight is the literate dialogue with characters quoting everyone from Marmee in *Little Women* to Wendy Steiner's *The Scandal of Pleasure: Art in an Age of Fundamentalism*."
—*Los Angeles Times*

"No one has a sharper eye than Amanda Cross."
—*The Washington Post Book World*

"Cross is wise in the ways of academe, and her figures speak in literate, complete sentences, which surely is a requirement for nuanced ambiguity."
—*The Boston Globe*

Please turn the page for more reviews. . . .

By Amanda Cross:

THE THEBAN MYSTERIES
POETIC JUSTICE
DEATH IN A TENURED POSITION*
IN THE LAST ANALYSIS
THE JAMES JOYCE MURDER*
THE QUESTION OF MAX*
SWEET DEATH, KIND DEATH*
NO WORD FROM WINIFRED*
A TRAP FOR FOOLS*
THE PLAYERS COME AGAIN*
AN IMPERFECT SPY*
COLLECTED STORIES*
THE PUZZLED HEART*

*Published by Ballantine Books

THE
PUZZLED
HEART

Amanda Cross

BALLANTINE BOOKS • NEW YORK

A Ballantine Book
Published by The Ballantine Publishing Group
Copyright © 1998 by Carolyn G. Heilbrun

All rights reserved under International and Pan-American Copyright Conventions. Published in the United States by The Ballantine Publishing Group, a division of Random House, Inc., New York, and simultaneously in Canada by Random House of Canada Limited, Toronto.

Grateful acknowledgment is made to Harvard University Press and the Trustees of Amherst College for permission to reprint an excerpt from Poem #43 from *The Poems of Emily Dickinson*, Thomas H. Johnson, ed., Cambridge, Mass.: The Belknap Press of Harvard University Press. Copyright © 1951, 1955, 1979, 1983 by the President and Fellows of Harvard College.

www.randomhouse.com/BB/

Library of Congress Catalog Card Number: 98-93527

ISBN 0-345-41884-0

Manufactured in the United States of America

First Hardcover Edition: January 1998
First Mass Market Edition: January 1999

10 9 8 7 6 5 4 3 2 1

To the very young cousins, Penelope and Matteo,
happily puzzled by almost everything

Could go from scene familiar
To an untraversed spot—
Could contemplate the journey
With unpuzzled heart—
       —FROM POEM #43
      EMILY DICKINSON

One

KATE FANSLER'S arrival on Leslie Stewart's door-step was thoroughly uncharacteristic.

Leslie Stewart was, at the moment the doorbell rang, trying to persuade one grandson not to pull out the cat's hair in handfuls and the other grandson, happily ensconced in a high chair, to put his applesauce to internal rather than external uses.

"Will you see to the door, Jane?" she called in what she hoped were plaintive rather than irritable tones. "I'm rather tied up here."

And indeed, Leslie thought, I would far rather be literally tied up or in almost any other situation but this. Grandchildren she cherished, but only, it came to her with sudden clarity, at their more adorable moments and in anticipation of departure, either theirs or hers as the case might be. Today, unfortunately, the case was neither.

"Jane," she called again. She could hear, then, a growl of acquiescence and Jane's footsteps as she crossed the loft to the front door, whose bell had again sounded, this time with urgency.

Jane Berlin had long liked to point out that she had remained childless for good reason and had fallen in love with Leslie when she too seemed well past the possibility of childbearing. It was the likelihood of grandchildren that she had failed to take into account. Apparently, having passed one's genes on to one generation, one felt impelled to encourage, even to assist, in the flowering of those genes into yet another generation. Jane felt, in a word, betrayed. *Outraged* was another word that might, without exaggeration, be employed. The strength of her feelings was in no way mitigated by Leslie's assurance that she agreed with her, and that this particular occasion was unavoidable and not likely to be repeated.

Jane's far-from-rapid progress was, toward the end, and at the bell's second ring, hastened by the happy thought that perhaps this was the boys' parents returning. She was almost smiling when she threw open the door.

Kate Fansler stood on the doorstep, looking so harassed that Jane did not even think to mention her disappointment in Kate's failure to be the retriever of the children.

"Are you all right?" Jane asked, somewhat rhetorically, since Kate looked far from all right. "Leslie's in the kitchen preventing cruelty to animals and swathed in baby food." Concerned, Jane followed Kate to the kitchen.

Leslie looked up in surprise. "What is it?" she said, clearly expecting the worst. And with reason. For Leslie, Kate's closest friend, knew that, in the first place, Kate never dropped in, never appeared unannounced, considering such behavior uncivilized; and, in the second place, would certainly not have chosen this afternoon to change in this respect since Leslie had told Kate of her, Leslie's, obligation to babysit for her grandsons. Kate was notorious for her lack of delight in the very young.

These thoughts were the matter of a few seconds. Abandoning the children, she went to Kate and pushed her into a chair. "I'll make some tea," she said. "Strong and sweet, for shock." And she did move toward the kettle.

"I'll do it," Jane said. "Unless you two would rather be alone."

"Reed's gone," Kate said.

"Left you?" Jane asked. Leslie glared at her.

"Not left me. Gone, vanished—kidnapped, if you insist on an exact description."

Even the boys were quiet, as though sensing the tension. Then the baby began to cry, his mouth turned down in the image of tragedy, his eyes scrunched up. The eyes of the older boy, as though in sympathy,

3

welled up; a tear rolled slowly down his cheek. The cat departed, not caring for the atmosphere.

Jane put up the kettle and waited for the water to boil. Personally, she would have recommended brandy, but perhaps Leslie was right. Leslie, being older and subject to more frequent familial perils, had dealt with crises more often than had Jane.

"Start at the beginning," Leslie said. She and Kate had seen each other through many trials, though it seemed to Leslie that laughter more often marked their conversations. They would begin in despair and end in laughter—that was about the size of it— but nothing, not even Leslie's losing her husband and taking up with a woman, had seemed as daunting as this. Pray heaven that Reed, the most unlikely man for it, had not had one of those male life crises and run off with a younger woman or, she suddenly thought, a man. Good God.

"We were to meet at a restaurant at six-thirty; we were going on to a concert at Lincoln Center. Reed is never late, or never really late, so after a time I called the lobby of our building to ask the doorman if perhaps Reed had forgotten and was planning to meet me there. The doorman said he hadn't seen Mr. Amhearst all day."

By this time the tea was ready, but Kate could barely be persuaded to take even a sip. "It's hot," she said.

"That's the point," Leslie said. "Do sip it at least." Kate, obeying, sipped.

By this time the boys had become more vocal in

their sorrows. Jane gathered them up; holding the baby on one arm, the older boy by the hand, she left the room with them.

Grateful, and terribly worried about Kate, Leslie nonetheless had the horrible thought that she would have to pay for this. I am becoming a monster, she told herself. "Go on," she said to Kate.

"Then I called the law school. His assistant Nick, a pleasant young man whom I've met, seemed surprised to hear from me. 'Actually,' he said, 'I watched Reed go, from the window; he had said he was going to a concert with you, and I thought how nice, when I would have to spend the evening studying. Then he got into the limousine and drove off.'

" 'What limousine?' I naturally asked. Reed calls limousines only for rides to the airport. Nick said he thought the men in the car had been waiting for Reed and were giving him an arranged-for lift. He didn't recognize the men, and when I told him that Reed was supposed to have met me at the restaurant, he became silent. 'Don't make too much of this, Kate,' he said, 'but now that you mention it, I did notice that the men got on either side of him and seemed to be, well, helping him into the limousine. It wasn't obvious, or I would have done something. I just think, looking back, that it was, well, funny. Can I do something, Kate?' I told him to hold off for a while and say nothing at all to anybody. He very nicely said he would be home all night if I needed him, he would go home instead of to the library."

Kate almost automatically sipped again at the tea. "After that call I went home. It was now perhaps seven-thirty. I didn't know what to do; every idea I had seemed less practical than the last. By nine o'clock I had about decided on some more telephone calls, when a message was delivered. That was a whole twelve hours ago; I still haven't thought what to do. The letter told me to be at home tonight at seven. Meanwhile," Kate concluded, "I'm here. I didn't know where else to go. I was afraid if I stayed home I would call the police or feel compelled to do something, anything, and I thought I'd better talk it through first. But maybe I should get back."

Leslie had never seen Kate so worried, so indecisive, so panicked. "I'd better go," Kate said. "I ought to be where someone can reach me. It was silly of me to come, but if I had to do something sudden and idiotic, this seemed the best choice."

"It was," Leslie said. "We'll go back together. I'll just have to get my daughter and her husband to come for the kids."

"It's all right," Jane said, appearing at the kitchen door. "They're changed and dressed now and can hang out with the less experienced of their two grannies, as Leslie's daughter calls us." Here she smirked. "It occurred to me while changing and dressing them that if Leslie's daughter were homophobic, she wouldn't have dreamed of leaving her little ones with us. Enough to make a cat laugh, isn't

6

it? You two go ahead to Kate's house, after Leslie calls the parents. I'll stay here till they come, trying to prevent serious injury to animals and children."

"Jane," Leslie began.

"Never mind Janeing me," Jane said. "Just call the parents and tell them to get on their bicycles and pedal over here."

"Wait a minute," Kate said. "You must have taken the kids for a good reason. Don't let—"

"And I'm giving them back for a good reason," Leslie said. "Nobility has its limits, and they've just been reached. Listen," she added, as Kate looked dubious and worried, "after a certain time in life, friends come first. Perhaps they should always come first. I was just trying to give the harried parents some much-needed time off, remembering my own years of child raising. But Jane hasn't taken my offer well, to put it mildly, so Tony and Sarah might as well find out how the land lies now as later. Actually, you're doing me a favor, giving me a good reason to back out now. Jane comes before grandchildren too, any day. Just let me have a word with her. Try to drink a bit more of the tea."

Dutifully Kate dropped back into her chair and tried to sip the tea, now cooler but still overpoweringly sweet. She too remembered from somewhere, English novels perhaps, that sweet strong tea was good for shock.

* * *

"Was that all the letter said?" Leslie asked when they were in a cab on their way to Kate's apartment. "Just to be home at seven?"

"For another message, I supposed," Kate said. "Letter or telephone. The other letter was hand-delivered. I asked the doorman, who said it was given him by a boy—obviously hired for the job, no connection to the kidnappers likely."

Leslie paid the cab and hurried after Kate into her apartment house. Kate was interrogating the doorman, who said that nothing had been delivered for her except the usual mail. Hurrying upstairs, they found the "usual mail" on the doorstep. Kate flipped through it; there was nothing unexpected or pertinent.

"Let's sit down," Leslie said. "I think you'd better start at the beginning. Have you the slightest idea why anyone would kidnap Reed? Some disgruntled criminal from Reed's D.A. days, out of prison and bent on revenge? An angry student; a disappointed client from one of his law school clinics; what?"

"It's me," Kate said. "It's because of me."

Leslie looked dubious.

"I've been warned," Kate said. "I guess you could say I've been picked as the feminist who's being taught that feminism doesn't pay. I've had warnings from some right-wing group, with one of those names—you know, the Institute for Family Values or something, the League for the Protection of Men. I forget what they were called. Anyway, they sounded crazy; I didn't take them seriously."

8

"These people shoot doctors who perform abortions," Leslie said. "They say God told them to do it."

"I know. I thought the warning was about me, they were going to do something to me. And I couldn't think what they could do except murder me, and I could hardly prevent that. As to whispering campaigns and false information to the media—that sort of thing—well, I wasn't going to stop living my life on that account. I never dreamed. . . ."

"Of course you didn't. How many warnings were there?"

"Several. I didn't pay that much attention. Something called the League of Right-Wing Women wrote diatribes against everything I've worked for. They seemed to be in favor of sexual harassment, battering women, date rape, and child abuse. Perhaps that's a bit strong. But they certainly don't believe any of these things happen on a large scale, and saying they do is all a plot to harry men. Leslie, I just thought they were crackers. In addition, I thought they were probably sending those warnings to many women. I didn't take it all that personally. The letter last night made it very personal."

"Let me see it," Leslie said.

Kate, who had held on to her purse, now took the letter from it and handed it to Leslie, who read it aloud:

We have taken your husband. If you do not publicly recant your insane feminist position, he may

9

come to harm. Be at home tonight at seven when further more detailed instructions will reach you. Do not contact the police or anyone else if you hope to see your husband alive again.

Leslie let the letter drop into her lap. "Kate, don't hit me, but is there any chance this is a joke? A stupid joke, in frightfully bad taste, but a joke. Some of those academic types you work with might think this was sort of funny; you know, the types who go off in the woods, pee against trees, and pretend to shoot each other."

"There's nothing I haven't thought of during the night," Kate said. "I don't think it's a joke, and the reason I don't is the two men Nick saw putting Reed into the limousine. Some of the guys I work with might try to frighten me, but they would find a time when Reed was away, or they'd think up some other prank. I can't believe they would actually force him into a car, that they would go that far, and then send this letter."

"It does seem to be the kind of letter they might write though. It's like kid stuff."

"Leslie, the right wing in this country, Christians though they may call themselves, are besotted with their message. They are like fundamentalists everywhere, certain of their correctness and of being ordered by God to destroy those who disagree with that certainty. I think perhaps we should stop fooling ourselves about them."

10

"I'm not fooling myself about them. I'm just saying that it's not that easy to distinguish that letter from a joke letter, the kind of anonymous note sent by nuts."

"I might agree with you if Reed were here. If I had heard from him, or had the slightest idea where he was. Now that I think of it, it was my certainty that I wouldn't hear from him that allowed me to go to you. I'm so frightened. And I feel so helpless."

"Which," Leslie said, "is why we have to get help. The question is who and how. Let's come up with several possible plans while we're waiting for seven o'clock—and their next message."

By the time they had reached this point, Kate was somewhat calmer, a bit more collected, though still capable, Leslie was certain, of collapsing into despair at the slightest provocation. Most ominously of all, she refused a drink, as though, Leslie surmised, Reed was doomed if Kate had a drink without him. By the time seven o'clock came around, and the doorbell rang announcing the delivery of the next message, Leslie had decided that coping with this kind of suspense required a wholly new, and for her unpracticed, support. Thinking of her grandchildren—by now, she hoped, claimed by their parents—she decided that life was never empty of new challenges, but with age one might have the fortitude to resist or meet them. Having, when push came to shove, resisted the grandchildren, she now sat with Kate hoping for the necessary fortitude.

The seven o'clock message demanded that Kate

announce, through paid advertisements or articles or op-ed pieces in specific newspapers and journals by the time of their next publication, why she was abandoning feminism and joining the right wing in its efforts to restore true family values. A list of the publications and a concise but terrifying definition of "family values" was appended. If Kate failed to comply with these demands, Reed would be killed. The message concluded: *Neither the police nor any government agency must be contacted*.

"I hate people who use contact as a verb," Kate said. It was, Leslie considered, the first sign that her mind had clicked back into place.

"I thought these people believed in the police," Leslie said, hoping to encourage this rational bent. "Or is that only for inner cities and against black men and boys?"

"We have to do something," Kate said.

"You don't think they'll kill Reed, not really?" Leslie asked. It struck her that this conversation horribly resembled one of those prime-time programs she occasionally watched when overcome with exhaustion.

"They've killed doctors who do abortions; they're fanatics. But it's not a very sensible demand. What's to stop me from denying the whole thing once Reed is back?"

"That's easy. In the first place, you'll be tarred with what you said, no matter what explanation you offer. That's how the media work. You can't ever correct reporters' misstatements, they just go on making them

12

anyway. In the second place, fear for Reed will restrain you. And if it doesn't restrain you, it will be because Reed insists it shouldn't, and that will lead to further complications of a marital sort. No, they're clever all right. It's always easy to be clever if compassion is not part of your aim. Just think about the way Pat Buchanan's mind works, or Rush Limbaugh's, and you'll have a good sense of what you're dealing with, even though neither of them has anything to do with this particular caper. Kate, are you listening?"

"Listening and thinking, along the same lines. Thank you for coming home with me, Les. I've just had a thought."

"Thank God for that. Do you plan to share it?"

"I think I know where to go for help, or at least for an initial conference. There's a woman I met last year named Harriet. I'll phone her."

"Don't phone. Give me a message and I'll deliver it. In these days of cyberspace, I don't trust any phone. If I'm being paranoid, better safe than sorry, as my mother used to say."

Kate wrote out the note.

Two

WHEN Harriet Furst arrived in response to Kate's note, Kate realized that it was far too long—months—since she had seen her. They had met while both were engaged in a more or less temporary capacity at the Schuyler Law School,* Kate in an unfamiliar role in unfamiliar surroundings, Harriet having taken on a new life and a new identity, which seemed to have propelled her wonderfully into the later decades of life. The friendship the two had formed was a lasting one, but they were both busy and neither, Kate realized sadly, had recently called the other. She mentioned this to Harriet.

"Well, here I am, in answer to a billet-doux. Better

*See Amanda Cross, *An Imperfect Spy*

14

than a phone call, really. What's the matter, my dear, and what can I do?"

"I thought perhaps you and your fellow private eye might help me. Harriet, I really don't know what to do."

"Start at the beginning—which was when?" Harriet said.

"Last night. And it seems like each hour has been a week long." Forcing herself into an appearance and voice of greater calm than she felt, Kate told Harriet the whole story thus far, which hardly took six sentences. Harriet listened with close attention.

"Now tell me about how you came to join a detective agency," Kate added. She did not analyze if her motive was to stall (action being dangerous) or to decide whether or not to trust Harriet in her new profession.

"Don't you think we'd better call Toni, my partner, and get her over here?"

"Yes. Meanwhile, tell me how all this happened. Of course, you are the perfect private eye."

"That's what Toni said about me. 'You're able to move about the world unseen, with the invisibility that age bestows in our society,' she said. I thought that rather clever of her."

"How did you meet her? Answering an ad?"

"Hardly." Harriet, after a long look at Kate, decided that talking was the most helpful activity she could undertake while they waited. "Toni (her full name is Antonia, I had hoped after the Willa Cather

15

novel, but Toni said not)," Harriet began, "had worked in the computer and Xerox copier room that, as you will vividly remember, I ran in that dreary law school. I hadn't seen her since I left there, but suddenly she turned up, offering me a job in a detective agency. The agency was to consist of Toni and me, and if it worked out, in a year or so I would be a partner. Of course I looked at Toni with some bemusement as she laid out this proposition. We were meeting in the office Toni had hired for her new undertaking. It was small and looked exactly like a private detective's office, my idea of which, perhaps like Toni's, had come from movies and TV shows about male detectives. There were two desks, two chairs besides the desk chairs, a rather grubby window, and a filing cabinet. One of the desks boasted a notebook computer, a telephone, and a fax machine. The other seemed to be waiting, hopefully I thought, for its occupant to arrive." Harriet paused to smile sympathetically at Kate before continuing.

"What really astonished me most about the whole business was Toni's looks—well, not so much her looks as her clothes and makeup. When I had known her at the law school, she had been thin and rather gawky, dressed always in jeans and, depending on the weather, either a T-shirt or a sweatshirt, both oversize. She now looked like something they might feature in one of those magazines devoted to fashion and the way to get yourself up if you want everyone to look at you with either admiration or horror. I was certainly looking at Toni. Her thinness had become elegance. Her clothes, even to my ignorant eye, were smashing in their expensive simplicity; they, together with her makeup and hairstyle, managed to convey simultaneously a come-on and a don't-mess-with-me message. The whole getup was staggering.

" 'Like it?' Toni said. 'I've done myself over. This is a power suit, in case you didn't know.' 'I didn't,' I said.

" 'Of course *you* mustn't feel guilty,' Toni said, seeing me dismayed at the fact that I hadn't changed an iota. 'I want you to look just like you look. That's part of the point of my offer—the way you look, your age, your cleverness, the way you handled all those frightful law school professor bullies, the fact, as you so often pointed out, that nobody even sees old women, let alone is able to describe them. All that's what I want. How about it?'

"Well, what did I have to lose? An adventure is an adventure. I even quoted her a poem I'd recently come upon by Sharon Barba called 'The Cycle of Women':

> Until she rises as though from the sea
> not on the half-shell this time
> nothing to laugh at
> and not as delicate as he imagined her
> a woman big-hipped, beautiful, and fierce.

"I wanted to add *old* in that last line, but it's not my poem. Still, that was me: big-hipped, old, and fierce.

"So we settled down to be a detective agency. It

17

was clear from the beginning that we were the perfect pair of operators. Toni got their attention and I worked where their attention wasn't. We followed errant wives, husbands and lovers, and missing children. That part was pretty grim; they were mostly teenagers who didn't want to go home when found, but at least the parents and the child were forced to talk to one another, which often hadn't happened much before." Here Harriet paused for another look at Kate, who smiled weakly, attempting reassurance.

Harriet continued. "Toni insisted we each have a licensed handgun. I refused, hating guns, but in the end I agreed, figuring I could always stash the thing in my capacious purse and never use it. I was wrong about that. We were hired by a boyfriend to tag along, unseen of course, with a young woman jogger who insisted on running just at dawn. I said I didn't think we undertook bodyguard work, but Toni said she ran anyway, and if the guy paid our rates, why not? So Toni ran when the girlfriend ran, and it's very likely that her being in sight and looking as though she could be carrying a gun discouraged a few rapists. All I know is that one day Toni couldn't make it, because of another case, and told me to go with her.

" 'Are you out of your mind?' I asked with my usual tact and gracious circumlocution.

" 'Get a bicycle,' Toni said. 'You can ride a bicycle, can't you?' I admitted that I could.

" 'Well,' she said, as though that ended the conversation.

" 'Well, okay,' I said, preserving my dignity. To give Toni her due, she provided the bicycle, one of those things with ten or twenty or so speeds, which I have never understood. But I can pedal, and I did. Round and round the park we went. The jogger stuck to the road, thank God, and if she wondered why this old bag was bicycling more or less along with her, she probably decided I was clinging to her for safety. People who run at dawn don't wonder too much about people who bicycle at dawn, or so I figured. And then he struck. He must have thought I wasn't any danger to him, since I was clearly aged and breathing heavily—I admit it, there were a lot of hills—and he pounced on her and dragged her beyond some bushes. I left the bicycle to its fate and followed, slowly and carefully. I was able to creep up behind him and put my gun to his head, just the way Louise did when Thelma was about to be raped in *Thelma and Louise*. 'Leave her alone,' I said. He looked so unconvinced that I shot the damn thing just past him, to make my point. He got the message, and tried to run off, but she tackled him, and I held him there while she went to call the police. One rapist off the park roads, or so we hoped. I rather enjoyed just holding the gun on him while he contemplated rushing me. 'Don't even think about it,' I said. 'I've got an itchy trigger finger.' Well, I had to get my dialogue from somewhere. I may have been a bit of a spy at the law school, but I'd never been a detective.

"The boyfriend gave us a bonus, but the woman

was mad as hell, which I thought unreasonable. Still, that wasn't our problem. And it was just about then that I became a partner, though we still called the agency by Toni's name, Giomatti. I didn't see any point in putting my name on the door."

"Anonymity has always attracted you," Kate said kindly, but glancing at her watch. Just then the phone rang. Kate answered, clearly frightened, but it was Toni. Kate handed over the phone.

"She wants you to go to school tomorrow in the usual way," Harriet said after a moment. "Either Toni or I will come to see you in your office hour; we'll have thought of a reason for doing so. Toni doesn't believe in being seen too often, in her undisguised self, with a client, not at first anyway. Sometimes I wonder, but she does seem to know what she's doing—as with the gun. I pointed out that an unloaded gun would have done as well. 'No it wouldn't,' Toni said, 'because you would have known it was unloaded and that would have made a difference.' She was right there.

"Now, Kate," Harriet continued, "let's have a drink. I know it's early, but you need one, and I need one. Reed wouldn't mind; I'm sure he's hoping you can get all the courage you need, even if the littlest bit of it comes from a bottle."

Kate rose to get the drinks. Harriet sat waiting, believing in the recuperative agency of even the most moderate exertion.

* * *

And so the next day Kate sat in her office dealing with students. It was an effort to force herself to concentrate on their concerns, but her success in doing so relieved the tension about Reed for a few minutes at a time. The sixth student, looking so natural in that persona that even Kate was fooled for a few minutes, was Toni, whom Kate vaguely remembered from the law school. Obviously Harriet's partner was talented at disguises, capable of assuming any costume and behavior consistent with her age and sex, and perhaps beyond. She looked exactly like a graduate student.

"I'm the last on line, I think," she said, taking the seat by the desk and staying in her role until the door was closed. "Thank God you don't teach in one of those small colleges where everyone in the place knows all the students personally. New York, I love you."

Kate looked questioning.

"Okay," Toni said. "Down to plans. I was going to mention, however, that we thought of Harriet as a cleaning woman come to dust, but were informed that a cleaning woman dusting during the day or for that matter at any other time would almost certainly arouse suspicions. So it's me, but Harriet sends love. We've been thinking about your case all night. Here's where we are for the present.

"First, rules of operation. Never telephone. If you absolutely must reach us, call from a phone booth on the street, give us the number, and we'll go out to a

21

street phone and call you back. Wait there for us. If someone else wants to use the phone, just stand there holding the receiver, keeping the lever down in an unnoticeable way. If someone bullies you out of the booth, just stay till you get in again. We'll keep trying. Is that clear?"

Kate nodded, trying to think where the phone booths were near her house or office. She realized how seldom she had used one, and planned to scout them out on her way home. Unobtrusively, of course. She still felt sick to her stomach, but less so now that some action was promised.

Toni continued: "We have lots of other plans, but I don't see any point in going into them all now. I'll be back during your office hours. I've signed up, with a late fee, for one of your courses so that I'll have a right to be here, particularly since I have to consult you often in order to catch up."

"Which course?" Kate asked.

"The big lecture. I don't want a grade, so I don't have to write papers or take a section with a student aide. I don't want them—the people behind this caper—to spot me as a student, but if they do, we can use that for our own purposes. Phony name, of course, but I paid money and I'm not matriculated, so they won't go into my records until later. Believe me, money is all, here as elsewhere." She continued before Kate could question any of this. "Our immediate problem is this ad or article they want you to place. You may have to do it, but right now we want

22

to stall them—partly because by stalling we force them to make some moves, and moves always tell you something, and partly because we don't want you to have to place the damn thing at all."

"But won't Reed be in danger?"

"I doubt it. Remember, Kate, he's only of use to them alive and well. They're planning one of two maneuvers, or so Harriet and I guess. Either they'll try to brainwash him and make him see the point of view of his captors, which often works very well indeed, or they'll try to seduce him—both mentally and physically, so prepare yourself for that. If Reed is half as smart as I hear he is, none of this is going to work, exactly, but he's going to pretend it does."

"You're remembering the abortion doctors they've shot, and the clinics they've bombed, and all that?"

"Look, Kate, forget abortion doctors and clinics. They feel morally right about that. They tell themselves they're saving human beings; they can use fanatics to do their dirty work for them. But these people aren't terrorists like the Islamic terrorists—they can't really claim that their god has told them to blow up the enemy even at the cost of lives. It still says 'Thou shalt not kill' in their Bible, and while the morality of killing abortion doctors—who also kill, in their view—or killing in time of war can be argued, kidnapping and killing is another kettle of fish. Are you with me?"

"I'm trying to be. I'm also remembering Yitzhak Rabin."

"Who was, like the abortion doctors, killed in a public place. Try to pull yourself together, Kate. You're no use to us or Reed if you're always in a panic, believe me."

"I'll try. How do I stall my refutation of feminism?"

"We thought of you having a minor heart attack: nothing life-threatening, if properly cared for, but requiring two weeks at least in bed. Don't start protesting. We abandoned that plan, not because we couldn't overcome your protests if we had to, but because your not teaching for two weeks doesn't send the right message. Anyhow, we need you here for consultations; we can't come to your home, or Harriet might come as a friend offering consolation but not more than once or twice. No, we're going to be simple and, to a degree, honest. You're going to put an ad in the paper, since you don't know how to get in touch with them, an ad saying: 'Need a week at least to write what you require.' Sign it Mrs. A. They'll get it, and with any luck no one else will."

"And at the end of the week?"

"We'll either have Reed back or regroup. Now listen. I've got the ad ready for the papers where they'll see it. They can't very well object if they want your conversion to fundamentalist Christianity to be believable. We'll also give Reed a chance to act on his own behalf."

"How? He's a prisoner."

"True. But he's not what they want, except insofar as he will work to influence you. It's feminism they're after, Kate, all the new laws about domestic violence, affirmative action, Title IX, choice, and let's throw in evolution and the idea that God may not be a man who created this world and meant men to be at the center of it. If Reed can appear to become impressed enough by their arguments, he will be working from the inside. You still with me?"

"I'm listening," Kate said. "You're not suggesting that he is likely to become swayed by their arguments?"

"No, I'm not. Pay attention, Kate. We're talking about a man you've been married to a lot of years. Are you asking *me*?"

"No," Kate said, sounding unconvincing even to her own ears.

"While you'll go on living your life, and supposedly pondering the article you're going to write as they demand," Toni went on, leaving in abeyance the question of Reed's compliance, "Harriet and I are going to try to identify the group that's taken Reed. That may not be as hard as you think, though it won't be easy."

"Where do you start?"

"We start, since we have to start somewhere, with a letter that appeared in the college newspaper damning feminists, multiculturalism, evolution, and the abandonment of family values. You may remember it caused quite a furor."

"I do remember. I couldn't imagine anyone being stupid enough to want to make it public. There was some question about why the paper published it, but

25

freedom of speech always wins out as an ideal, and in this case it probably should have. When it's racial slurs in an academic community, I'm not always so sure, but that's another subject for a quieter time."

"Right," Toni said. "But I'm glad to see your mind grapple with something other than Reed's disappearance."

"Kidnapping. That's what I can't get over. Actually kidnapping a grown man to get even with a woman whose ideas you don't much like."

"Let's not go round this again. Not now—okay, Kate? I'm off. You know what Garrison Keillor says every week on public radio: be well; do good work; stay in touch." And Toni was gone, slouching out of the office in superb imitation of a student whose essay had not received the accolade she thought it deserved.

Harriet turned up that night at Kate's apartment. "We are friends," she explained. "You weren't supposed to tell anyone, so life goes on, right, and your old friends come by to see you? Right? And though it's supposed to look like it, this isn't just a friendly visit. I want to tell you the next step. We'll keep in touch, mostly through Toni-the-student, so don't fret. That is, I know you can't help fretting, but don't fret about our keeping in touch. Any single malt on hand?"

Kate went to fetch it, but didn't this time feel up to

a drink for herself—a terrible symptom, but Harriet decided to ignore it. She herself took a grateful sip.

"We've looked into the background of the college student who wrote that letter to the paper. Always begin with the obvious. That's the place to begin, if not to end. He turns out to be the dutiful son of a widow who thinks every law to help women, the poor, blacks, or anyone else other than the white male holy Christians of this world is the work of the devil. Satan figures rather largely in all this. (Have you read Elaine Pagels on the subject? Well, never mind that for now.) I'm finding this private detective business wonderful, but you do have to keep to the point and your mouth shut—hard tasks for longtime talkers like me. Where was I?" Harriet held out her glass. "And don't ask if it's all right to drink on the job. It isn't, but I'm considering this a friendly visit. I shall breathe heavily at the doorman as I leave, convincing him that I've been having a nice, boozy time."

Kate attempted a smile. "Go on," she said, "about the family of the boy who wrote the letter."

"As I say, spiritual pride is clearly not among what that family considers sin; they know they are always right. But we found out that one of the daughters got captured by a cult, and the other one has lived a life that is, I gather, unacceptable to Mama in every possible way. However, the son is his mother's boy. Papa, by the way, was a minister who died some years ago of a coronary. I get whispers of the fact that his

27

sexual tastes, which ran to the young and male, were not exactly according to the book, but that has all been hushed up. It goes a certain distance, though, together with the careers of the daughters, in explaining the righteousness of the mother and son. We may get around to cultivating the mother, who is trying to start a movement, which I might join. That may not lead anywhere, but who knows? Meanwhile, your ad goes in all possible journals and papers tomorrow. We shall await results. If you get any messages or communications of any sort, bring them to your office hour."

"Suppose it's not a day for my office hour?"

"I was coming to that. Patience, Kate; do try. You're going to get a puppy. Just sit down and listen, please. A nearly three-month-old puppy greatly in need of training, not to mention shots and all the rest of the usual attentions from a vet. We've found you an excellent vet, by the way, nearby. We've also managed to get a young man who does occasional work for us hired as a desk clerk there. People always need competent help; Ovido is very good, and speaks Spanish. There's a dog training center upstairs from the vet. When you go there, which is always on the days when you don't go to the university, if you have a message, leave it with Ovido. He will recognize you and take whatever it is unobtrusively, while discussing your dog's medication. Here's the address."

"And where is the dog?" Kate hardly dared ask.

She realized that for the first time she felt her life to be completely out of her control. That she might have a dog foisted on her seemed as likely as anything else that had been happening.

"The kennel will deliver the dog tonight. You will take her around to be examined by the vet after she arrives. She is paper-trained, by the way, so put some paper down in the kitchen. She does like to walk, however. She's going to be a very big dog—she's a Saint Bernard, in fact—weighing between a hundred and fifty and two hundred pounds, so early training is essential while you can still lift her and pull her, in short, while you're still stronger than she is."

Kate looked both blank and stricken.

"Kate dear," Harriet said, "I'm really worried. Talk to me. Ramble on. Quote things. Please, Kate, don't stay in this zombie state. Say something. Reed will be back, I promise you. The dog's name is Bancroft, by the way, because Anne Bancroft is a favorite actor of the kennel owner. Banny for short. She's a very sweet dog; I've seen her. Quite adorable, you'll see."

"And what am I do to with her when she weighs two hundred pounds?"

"Oh, we're just borrowing Banny. She's far too valuable to give away or even sell. She's wanted for shows and then for breeding. Now don't get too attached to her, because she's just visiting. You do see, Kate, don't you? We needed a place you could go regularly, quite innocently, where messages can be exchanged. Meanwhile Banny will learn how to sit,

29

lie, stay, heel, and fetch, and no doubt many other wonderful tricks. She's a present from me, by the way. But for God's sake, for my sake, don't let anything happen to her. That dog's worth a bundle."

Kate still looked stunned. "Harriet," she slowly said, "do you really know what you're doing?"

"We do, my dear, please try to believe that. We'll have Reed back before you know it. Goodbye for now. And look out for Banny; the kennel will deliver her shortly. The doorman will bring her up."

"I hope she doesn't pee in the elevator," Kate said.

"Ah," Harriet said, "that's more like it. Do have a drink," she said, as she left. "I know Reed would want you to."

Kate thought for a while, no coherent idea remaining in her mind for long. Time seemed to have lost its meaning; then the doorbell rang. There on the doormat stood the doorman with an adorable, furry thing with a wrinkled brow who looked as bewildered as did Kate. She took the leash.

"Here's some food they left for him," the doorman said. "I hope you enjoy him, ma'am. He's going to be a mighty big dog."

"It's a she," Kate said. "Thank you."

Kate and Banny were alone. Banny looked around, then squatted and peed on the foyer floor.

After Kate had cleaned that up and laid paper down in the kitchen and showed the paper to Banny and put some water down, she went back into the living room. The puppy jumped up against her knees, and on an impulse Kate picked up the bundle of fur, hugging it, and weeping onto it. The puppy licked her face.

Three

Kate, in order to set up the ordinariness of her visits to the vet and training class, went there with Banny over the weekend. At least it was something to do. She could spot Ovido behind the desk, and, while paying for the vet's examination of Banny, she chatted with him in a natural way so that, if she should have a message to leave, their conversation would not appear in any way different from her usual behavior.

Harriet and Toni were convinced she was being followed, and Kate had occasionally caught sight of someone who might well have been keeping her in sight. "Their main object is to frighten you," Toni had said, "so they want you to know you're being followed and hounded. But don't underestimate them.

Don't do anything you wouldn't do during your ordinary day." (Toni forbore to mention, and Kate did not point out, that no day would ever be ordinary again.)

On Monday, when she had a scheduled office hour, Kate took with her a message that had arrived the previous evening from the group that had kidnapped Reed; she did not need to go the route of the vet this time. The message said that the ad had been seen, and that Kate had exactly one week—that is, until next Monday—to place her article, which would be expected to appear not many days thereafter. If not, Reed would die or be terribly wounded.

Inevitably, this last caused Kate some bad moments, despite Toni's assurance that threats weren't what mattered at this point. Getting Reed back was all that mattered. Meanwhile, Toni went on to say, encouragingly, that she and Harriet were keeping a close record of everything that happened. "We shall be in a position to prosecute when this is all over. Meanwhile, we want you to do something."

"A cat this time?"

"Sarcasm is a nonproductive mode of communication," Toni said with pedagogical hauteur. "Listen, I don't want to stay longer than the other students and call attention to myself, so I won't go into all that Harriet and I are doing. Here's what we want you to do."

Kate looked both frightened and eager, a combination hard to achieve and terrible to experience.

"Don't look so appalled," Toni said. "This is an

interesting job. Harriet told you that one of the daughters leads what the mother and son consider an unacceptable life, and I've tracked her down. She doesn't seem to see much of her mother and brother, but I think she's not much in sympathy with them. She doesn't know about Reed; you will have to meet her more or less accidentally, and using your own judgment, tell her as much as you want. My hunch is that she may be able to help us."

"And how do I meet her?" Kate asked.

"Easy. She lives in Putnam County, where she runs a kennel and boards dogs. You and Banny will go and check it out. Here's the address and phone number. You take it from there. But remember, if you have the least doubt, keep it a visit about boarding dogs."

"Perhaps I should cut my class and office hour tomorrow and go to visit her."

"Absolutely not. Don't, whatever you do, change your normal habits. You can go after your class tomorrow. Call first to make sure she'll be there and that a visit of inspection is welcome. And don't forget to take Banny. When one questions dog owners, it's ever so much more convincing if you have a dog."

And so, the next day, after her class, Kate picked up the car from the garage and Banny from the apartment. She had called and been told she would be welcomed by the owner herself, Dorothy Hedge, daughter of the right-wing mother, sister of the son. "A Saint Bernard!" the owner had exclaimed. "What a brave woman you are. I raise Norwich terriers.

34

They love big dogs; I suspect they think they're big themselves. So come right along."

Kate parked Banny in the backseat, but it soon became clear that Banny had no intention of staying there. She squeezed through the space between the two front seats and plopped herself in Kate's lap. Kate pushed her onto the other front seat when they stopped for a light, and Banny tried putting just her head on Kate's thigh, but that interfered with the gearshift. So she went back to Kate's lap and flattened herself, more or less, under the steering wheel. It was far from a safe arrangement, but it had its comforts. Kate found herself talking to the dog, and checking the directions out with her.

Rather to her surprise, Kate found the right turn off the parkway, and after that it was just a matter of counting lights and then mailboxes. They pulled into Dorothy Hedge's driveway, clearly marked with a sign (HEDGE KENNELS), to a cacophony of barks punctuated by a cheerful female voice shouting "Quiet, quiet, you beasts," to no effect whatever.

As the owner of the voice approached them, Kate had the impression of someone enjoying herself in a ritual that had meaning only for the participants and was never meant to change immediate circumstances. Dorothy Hedge was a large, hearty woman, her booming voice natural, Kate felt, one that would be so even in a job that did not require it. She welcomed Kate with a vigorous handshake and Banny with some mild roughhouse. "Aren't you adorable," she said.

"I supposed that owners of dog kennels were rather restrained in their enthusiasm," Kate said, smiling. "How nice to see someone so frankly happy about dogs."

If Dorothy Hedge thought this a somewhat odd remark, she did not show it. "It's easy to be boisterous around dogs," she said. "They don't have principles, only affections and canine opinions about sensible things. Did you want to see the boarding facilities? Not," she added, "that I recommend boarding a dog this young, but doubtless you have your reasons. Around this way."

Kate found the boarding arrangements quite impressive, and had no trouble saying so. Each boarding dog had a large outdoor cage, attached to a much smaller sheltered area, a sort of lean-to doghouse.

"Once they're at home here, and unless they're particularly unfriendly types, I let my dogs run together in that big fenced-in area there. But not this little girl, I think; she's too likely to be bullied, or to feel frightened even if not bullied. Have you had her long?"

"No," Kate said. "And I don't plan to board her in the near future. But since I'm often called away suddenly, it seemed sensible to have all the arrangements in place for such an eventuality."

"Very wise. Too many people think they can dump dogs as though they were furniture or a package. The poor things get off their feed and mope. Now this little girl will have been here before, and she'll know you and I have met and talked. That matters. Would you like a cup of tea?"

"I'd love one, thank you," Kate said, happy to have been offered a chance for further conversation. Though how she was to get from dogs to this woman's bigoted mother she could not imagine. She followed Dorothy Hedge around to the door, but hesitated, with Banny at her heels.

"Oh, bring the baby girl," Dorothy said. "I just saw her do a wee-wee, so maybe we're in luck. Anyway, if I had a dollar for every time I'd wiped up dog pee, I'd be a wealthy woman, I assure you. Let's go into the kitchen and I'll make the tea."

It was a large, country kind of kitchen, and Kate sat at the table, taking Banny onto her lap after the puppy kept jumping up against her. "I know it's silly," Kate said, "but I wonder, if she sits in my lap now, will she expect to when she weighs over a hundred and fifty pounds?"

"Take her to training class, my dear, as soon as possible. She's got to learn to do what you say, and soon, before she's bigger than you are."

"We are enrolled in a training class," Kate said, feeling as though, like Alice, she had become quite a different person altogether, discussing dogs this way, "but so far we've mainly been doing standing-up things."

"Well, the command *down* will soon come into it.

Enjoy her, my dear. There are few more utterly satisfying things than a puppy. And she'll add a dozen years to your life."

But will she add years to Reed's life? Kate thought, but did not say. Dorothy, as she had asked Kate to call her, promising to call Kate Kate in exchange, poured the tea from a teapot around which was a knitted tea cozy. I have come to something out of *Country Life*, Kate thought, sipping her tea. Banny slept in her lap.

"What is it you really want from me, my dear?" Dorothy asked, sipping her own tea and savoring one of her own cookies. Kate had not felt up to trying one, afraid she might choke on it.

"What do you mean?"

"My dear Kate, if you have had that adorable puppy for more than a week, I'll eat my hat. You also don't know anything at all about boarding dogs; you haven't asked a single question, intelligent or not."

"I'm an observer," Kate said, rather defensively.

"I likewise. I don't know where you got Banny, but I'm willing to bet this house against your car that she's on loan. The question about her being in your lap as a big dog was cute, but, my dear, big dogs don't try to sit in your lap, any more than big people do. Little dogs are a different matter. But even my Norwich terriers have too much dignity to jump into anyone's lap, and they're not that enamored of being picked up either. All that might have been explained away, but it's clear you're a nervous wreck, and that you think there's some way I can help you. What is it? Do you want to leave Banny with me while you straighten out whatever mess landed you with her? I'll need some sort of contract, but I'm willing. Or is it something else? How did you hear of me anyway?"

Kate sat there, stroking Banny's soft fur. She had, it seemed to her, only two choices. She could get up and leave, or she could begin some sort of approach to the truth. The woman already knew her name. Perhaps it would be worth trusting her a little. After all, to leave would accomplish nothing.

"Let me help if I can," Dorothy said. "I looked you up in *Who's Who* before you came, assuming you're who you say you are. I find it a useful reference in this business, so don't look so surprised. You'd be amazed to learn how many people claim to be someone well-known when they arrive with a dog. Their motives are varied, but usually sordid. A few questions soon settle the matter. I'm ready to believe you're who you say you are, though you're not here for doggy reasons. What can I do for you?"

"I came about your brother," Kate said, feeling totally idiotic. She had never felt so powerless and devoid of personality in her life. It was a combination of despair, sorrow, anger, and helplessness, a wicked brew.

"My brother? Kenneth, the college boy? That's right, he's still matriculating at the place where you teach. Why didn't I think of that right off the bat? Kenneth's a bit late to be a college boy, but then he's always been backward about everything, a true mama's boy. Is he a student of yours?"

"No. I've never met him. He wrote a letter to the college newspaper."

"Ah, I see. Promulgating all the old family values and old-time morals, which mostly add up to supporting the rich, the male, and the white, though that's probably not the right order. Look, did you agree with his letter?"

"No. I thought it quite mad. But it did cause me a good bit of concern."

"My dear, of course it did. Ken is fifteen years younger than me, and thirteen years younger than my sister. He was an afterthought, and not a happy one, in my opinion. But he was male. My mother felt like Sarah: God had blessed her at last. My poor sister ended up in one of those cults where they tell you what to do and who to marry and what to think every minute of the day, exactly like home, I would have thought—but at least it wasn't home. She had got in the habit of being told what to think, I guess, and couldn't break it; I just got out. Our father died after Ken was born; I suspect he died of syphilis, except that no one seems to die of that anymore. Well, as you may gather, it's not your basic happy family. Whether it represents true family values, I don't know, but I suspect it does: general misery all around, unless you can join in the assurance that you are absolutely right about everything, no questions permitted. Tell me something about yourself."

"You know what's in the reference book. All I can tell you of any importance that isn't there is that I've acted, from time to time, as a detective. Purely amateur. But," Kate added, more to herself than to Dorothy, "my skills in that area seem to have gone with my self-confidence."

"Kate, my dear," Dorothy said, "you're obviously in some kind of trouble, and what that trouble is is none of my business. On the other hand, you came out here to see me with a puppy you seem to have acquired in the last twenty-four hours, so I may be allowed to assume that you haven't come about the dog. If it was primarily a kennel you wanted, there are others nearer the City—not as good, I admit, but adequate. Why did you come to me?"

"I've had her a few days, actually," Kate said, stroking Banny. "And I have to admit I'm hooked, although I don't think I'm going to be allowed to keep her." And to Kate's embarrassment, her eyes filled with tears.

"Let me put it this way," Dorothy said. "Either you're the greatest actress since silent films, or you're in deep trouble. Don't tell me if you just need to wail, not that I won't sympathize, but you'll just end up hating me and yourself for so uncharacteristic—I'm guessing—a confidence. But if you came here for a purpose, why don't we discuss what it is?"

"It's about your brother."

"Ken? You mean you do know him after all? Don't

tell me you're involved in any way with Kenneth, unless he's blackmailing you or trying to bully you into
giving him a passing grade. Otherwise, I shall have
misjudged you badly. Very badly."

There was a honking from outside. "Ah, the Car-
lisles, come for their bull terrier. And not a moment
too soon, I assure you. That dog gives new meaning
to the verb *to chew*. You just rest here, and think
about what you have to say and if you want to say it.
I'll be back soon."

Dorothy went out of the kitchen door. Kate could
hear voices in greeting, then a moment's silence, and
then human screams of welcome. Kate went to the
window and saw a dog with black spots leaping up
and down in joy, running to the man and woman
who had come to pick him up, then back to Dorothy
(quite a tribute that, Kate thought), then back to his
owners. Kate saw Dorothy present the man with
what was clearly a bill, since the man took out his
wallet, extracted a check, and made it out, leaning on
the fender of his car. Hands were shaken all around.

When the man opened the front door of his car, the
bull terrier leapt in and had to be dragged out and
forced into the backseat. "I'll sit with you, Doc," the
woman said, joining the dog in the backseat. Dorothy waved as the car pulled out.

I am certainly learning something about the dog
world I wouldn't have dreamed of knowing a few
days ago, Kate thought. I shall have to tell Reed. And
then the panic in her gut returned.

Dorothy came back in, pausing to place the check on a desk in the large kitchen. "Like so many dog owners, they are covered with guilt for undertaking any adventure that doesn't include Doc. Between those people who acquire dogs and then simply dump them, and those who treat them better than most people treat their children, I don't know which to condemn more. But at least this puts money in my pocket, and the dog doesn't suffer. I hate to see dogs suffer. Speaking of suffering—mine—let's take this little lady out now that she's woken from her nap. Pees follow sleep in puppies. Remember that, at least as long as you have this one."

Kate carried Banny outside. The dog immediately confirmed Dorothy's wisdom by squatting. Kate thought how nice it must be to know absolutely everything there was to know about one subject, even dogs. Literature, somehow, never lent itself to such assurance; detecting even less.

Suddenly, Kate remembered Harriet's telling her that she might well be followed everywhere. Had she been followed here? There was no sign of anyone, but if she had been seen entering this place, surely Dorothy's mother and brother would be suspicious that she had picked this particular kennel. Might it not be best to keep the visit as purely doggy as possible? On the other hand, Kate mused, if she was followed and they knew she had met Dorothy Hedge, why not take the opportunity to get Dorothy on her side. After all, if Dorothy were secretly in cahoots with her family, while denying she had anything to do with them, then she would know what was going on and would hardly need Kate to tell her. The only possible flaw in this reasoning would be if Reed's kidnappers were not in any way connected with Dorothy's family, if her family did not know of the kidnapping, and if Dorothy, secretly working with them, were to tell them the story, thus further endangering Reed. Somehow, this seemed too farfetched, even for Kate in her present mode of acute suspicion. She decided—not for the first time, she wryly told herself, but never wholly wrongly either—on trust.

Still, one might ask a question or two. Suppose this woman said, "I'm not a feminist, but I believe in equal pay." Would one want to trust someone capable of such an answer with help against a violently antifeminist group? No, Kate thought, probably not.

"What do you think of feminism?" Kate asked. If Dorothy thought that question odd, she gave no sign.

"What do I think of it? It saved my life, that's what I think of it. If I hadn't run into feminism when I did, I'd still be wondering why I felt my family to be so wrong when everyone else seemed to be on their side. Suddenly, everyone else didn't seem to be on their side. All that I'd been feeling, it turned out, others had been feeling; it was deliverance. Judging from the bits about you in *Who's Who*, I gather you're something of a feminist yourself. Am I wrong?"

"No," Kate said. "You're not wrong. I'm married, you see," she began.

44

"Yes," Dorothy said, "that was in *Who's Who* too."

"You see, my husband's been kidnapped. I hate the word *husband* but not so much as I hate the word *wife*. Still—"

"What do you mean, kidnapped?"

"Just that: forced into a car, taken away, held with threats to kill him if I don't within a few days write a piece, dramatic enough to be published, about why I am abandoning feminism forever. Therefore, I conclude that the kidnappers are right-wing types who loathe feminism, loathe and fear it."

"And you think Kenneth and Ma might be involved?"

"I've no reason to think so, but it's the only lead I've got. When I heard about you, I thought, well, it's worth a try."

"Is that why you borrowed the cuddly puppy?"

"No. That was for other reasons. But I have to tell you that someone may have followed me here. I didn't see them, but then I wasn't thinking of being followed; I should have been. I'm afraid my mental powers have not been exactly sharpened by all this."

"And why should they? I need time to think," Dorothy said. "I don't know how to find out if my family's involved, since I haven't talked to them in several years, but I'll think of something. Meanwhile, let's hope they followed you. If they did, they'll probably be in touch with me, and then we'll know who they are. I tell you what: you better leave Banny with me; that will give you a reason to come back. Let's say you asked me to house-train her for you."

"Oh, no," Kate cried, astonishing herself. "I can't leave Banny. I need her for other reasons I can't go into."

"And as a talisman and comfort. Okay. But it will make our communicating harder. I tell you what. Give me a day, and bring her back here Thursday evening. I should have something to report, or maybe nothing. If there's nothing, your coming here won't matter. If there's something, at least we can talk here then, and arrange somehow to meet somewhere else. Is it a date?"

"It's a date," Kate said, and with that she had to be content.

Four

B Y the time Kate took leave of Dorothy Hedge, the traffic on the Taconic and the Saw Mill Parkway had thickened. At each of the traffic lights on the Saw Mill, Kate was forced to stop, waiting impatiently for the cars ahead of her to move as the signal turned green. The powers that be had, thank whatever politician was responsible for so sensible a decision (and of course one did not know whom to thank; one seemed only to know in such matters whom to blame), removed the tollbooth on the Saw Mill Parkway, eliminating the worst of the bottlenecks. But soon afterward came the Henry Hudson Bridge, and long, long lines of those without tokens or E-ZPass waiting to pay the toll.

As Kate sat powerless in her car, she could feel her frustration rising. Banny, sensing her tenseness, awoke and licked Kate's face. It's the passivity of it, Kate thought, the powerlessness, the complete lack of control, the regimentation. Lines always did this to Kate, which was why she had long since got out of the habit of going to movies or patronizing the more fashionable restaurants. Enforced passivity.

But what exactly had Kate been indulging in, ever since Reed was taken, *but* passivity? She had first gone into a trance, then rushed over to Leslie's for comfort, then turned the whole thing over to Toni and Harriet. She had allowed herself to be given a dog—however appealing—and had used the dog for what action they had left her.

Reed had been kidnapped, and it was time, it really was time, she thought as she edged the car forward, for her to begin to think for herself, perhaps to act for herself. She was so overwhelmed by this realization that she forgot to move forward, and the driver in back of her honked irritably. She felt better, stroking Banny, who went back to sleep. She would put her mind to the matter, her mind rather than her emotions or her fears. Surely, however, it would be wise to consult someone, to bounce ideas off someone. Yes, she decided, she would call Leslie and confer with her. And the hell, up to a point, with Toni and Harriet's orders. She almost wished she had a phone in the car, an indulgence she had always considered the height of folly, necessary only for corporate lawyers and people who lived in California and spent a third of their life on one or another freeway.

By the time Kate had made it through the tolls and on to the garage, had left the car and walked home with Banny, now attached to her leash and collar, and stopped frequently to have Banny admired, touched, and cooed over, she was altogether determined upon action. She did not yet know of what kind, but she was resolved upon abandoning her passive despair, which might be forgiven as an initial response, but which had gone on far too long.

First Kate called Leslie to tell her she was feeling better, and that things were looking up a bit. "I've had it with sitting around, worrying, and doing nothing," Kate said. "But I don't want to go off half-cocked. What do you think?"

Leslie agreed that it was about time Kate took charge of the situation, and said that she, Leslie, was damn glad to hear it. She reported that her grandsons had returned home, and that she was at Kate's disposal anytime she was needed.

"I just wanted a friend's assurance that I hadn't taken leave of my senses," Kate said.

"You've got it," Leslie answered, "in spades." Kate promised to call back soon, hung up, then immediately lifted the receiver and called Harriet and Toni.

"I know you said not to call," Kate explained to an outraged Harriet, "but that is an order I've decided

49

not to obey. You are working for me, you and Toni, and I want to see you tonight. Here. I don't care if someone is watching me, or if they see you visiting, or if they wonder whether you're visiting as friends or detectives. We've got to talk. I'll expect you here for a drink at six." And Kate hung up amid howls of protest from Harriet. Six was less than an hour away, and Kate had some organized thinking to do.

When Harriet arrived, looking fit to be tied, as they used to say in Kate's youth and probably in Harriet's, she announced that Toni was not coming, since she didn't approve of this meeting. Harriet, it was always possible, might still be interpreted as a friend visiting in a difficult time. Kate had assembled the single malt Scotch, ice, and glasses, and was clearly prepared for action. She poured some Scotch and began talking.

Harriet opened her mouth to protest, but only, Kate noticed, after she had got some whiskey into it. Kate held up a silencing hand. "Listen to me," she said. "I've listened to you two for days, I've adopted a dog"—who, perhaps exhausted from her travels, was asleep in an armchair—"and now it's my turn to talk."

Harriet knew when argument would be futile and listening the only sensible response. She leaned back and assumed, with a sigh, a listening position.

"I've been thinking, starting from the beginning and analyzing the situation anew. My first observation is that, however closely the student who wrote that antifeminist letter may be connected with the radical right, he is not the only male chauvinist student around. No doubt you remember the boys at Cornell who wrote in favor of silencing women and having a free ticket to rape—they wrote on e-mail I think, but the means of broadcasting are immaterial." Harriet nodded that she did remember. "So," Kate continued, "I began thinking of students who might have objected to my course, or might think this sort of caper as funny as rape, if you follow me."

"Closely," Harriet said, sipping.

"Here's yet another example," Kate said, picking up a clipping and waving it at Harriet, who watched unperturbed. "In a 'Forum' discussion, 'Discouraging Hate Speech without Codes,' in *Academe*, the magazine of the AAUP, the American Association of University Professors." "I have heard of it," Harriet interjected mildly; Kate ignored her. "Professor Susan Gubar reports the following: 'What is to be done when I discover a note affixed to the office door threatening to disrupt a Women's Studies symposium on sexual violence or, most malevolently, I find a burn mark up and down the same door? What do I do if a student protests the one lecture spent on women's issues as "too much about feminism" by tearing the course pack up before the class? Or if one of my graduate students tells me she has received notes from a freshman who threatens to stalk her?' I'm just

51

reading you this," Kate added, "so that you'll see where I'm coming from."

"I've seen it long since," Harriet said. "But remember, Gubar teaches in Bloomington, Indiana, where they're a little less sophisticated."

"Exactly. They might not be sophisticated enough to think up a kidnapping scheme, but my students are; I just wanted to establish the facts in a general way."

"Consider them established."

"Okay. What I'm suggesting, as you've no doubt already guessed, is that this may well be a prank of some student, particularly the sort who belongs to a fraternity—an assumption based on what some of my women students have told me of assaults on them in fraternities—though not all fraternities, one hopes—and I intend to follow that lead as far as I can. For instance, who rented the limo into which Reed was forced?"

"Naturally Toni thought of that. She has already discovered the car was hired under a corporate arrangement a male undergraduate at your university's father has with a limo company."

"Nice of you to let me know," Kate interjected, "however ungrammatically."

Harriet ignored this. "A man called up and ordered the car, giving the name of the company and the number of the account. Of course," Harriet said, pausing maddeningly to refill her glass, "we interviewed the student in question. He turns out to be a wealthy, generous, rather laid-back guy who had been heard often ordering limos through his father's firm. But he didn't do this; someone else did, and he is certain it isn't one of his close friends. The company had nothing to add except that the car picked up two young men in midtown, took them up to the law school, waited for a 'friend,' i.e., Reed, and took them only a few blocks before it was dismissed. Toni has talked to the driver, who rather had the impression the passenger they picked up was requiring persuasion to get into the car and then to leave it, but it wasn't anything *heavy*—his word. So you see, my dear, we have got that far. But we still think the letter-writer was probably involved."

"Good," Kate said. "We have a meeting of minds then, which is always so encouraging. Now, I've decided a few things. First, no more of this secrecy and message game. That is, I think leaving messages at the dog place is a good idea, and we might as well continue with that. But I want to meet with you openly, and to be in on all the operations. Otherwise, I'll hire another firm."

"Toni wouldn't like it."

"So much the worse for Toni. I have a job for her, by the way."

"I don't think she'll like that either."

"Well, if she doesn't like it, I'll have to find another operator—is that the right term? I've a number of friendly students who will gladly take on the task, but there's some danger involved, and I'd rather have Toni, who looks the part *and* can handle trouble better than students. Will you tell her, or should I?"

"Let me tell her," Harriet said. "I might be a teeny bit more persuasive, under the circs."

"The what?"

"That's what the British used to call the circumstances in the good old days of Lord Peter and company. I suspect you haven't been keeping up with your literary reading."

"Not lately," Kate said, and really smiled for the first time since Reed's kidnapping.

"That's better. What is Toni's assignment, then, although I hardly dare ask?"

"I want her to get herself up looking both like a student and sexy. She'll know what I mean, and if she doesn't, tell her to rove around the campus and observe. Then I want her to visit all five fraternities. She needs a reason, subscriptions to a new magazine or flyers for a student production, something of that sort. I want her to case the joints. 'Gee, I've never been in a fraternity. Would you guys show me around, like where do you sleep and all?'—well, you get the picture. I think Reed may be being kept in one of those houses. Toni wouldn't be able to determine that on her first visit, but she'll get some idea of the layout and the possibility of keeping a prisoner there. And all this has to be done tomorrow, need I say?"

"Toni's going to love it, but I'll tell her orders are orders. She may want to talk to you."

"I've thought of that; if she does, let's use e-mail. It's totally insecure, and therefore we will be assumed not to use it. We will simply have to think of roundabout ways to say things."

"I didn't know you had e-mail."

"Of course I do. It's the best way of getting department notices without having to drop in and confront one's most tiresome colleagues. Here's my e-mail address," Kate said, handing Harriet a slip of paper.

"All right," Harriet said, taking it. "On your head be it. Well, tally-ho and all that, as they also said in the good old class-ridden days. Toni or I will report back real soon."

"Don't tally-ho quite yet, if you don't mind," Kate said. "I think I have a task for *you*, but I've got to dig up some information. Do you mind having another glass by yourself? I won't be long."

"A pleasure," Harriet said. "But don't dawdle."

Kate went into her study to look through her class lists from recent semesters. There was often a young man in one of her classes, and sometimes a young woman, who took offense at any mention of women's oppression or revolution, or the assignment of a book by a woman. This was, Kate had discovered after much suffering, not always because of "this feminist crap," as angry students had been known to call it. Women like Kate in positions of authority always evoked the mother in students' minds, and sometimes that was sufficient for a negative personal response, particularly when added to a general hostility on the part of students to seeing women in positions of authority and power. It occurred to Kate, not for the first time, that someone ought to write a manual on the dangers for women in teaching, with a chapter on women teachers who were no longer young.

Kate found names of four students who might have harbored resentment and nursed it sufficiently to have it flower into a kidnapping. She doubted, however, that such resentment would lead to actual danger for Reed. But, danger or not, it must be horrible to be kept a prisoner and to know why, for surely part of the fun would be in telling him he was suffering because he had her, Kate, for a wife.

On the other hand, Kate thought, if this really was a radical and probably mad fringe of the religious right, they might go further, as they so often had, even in academic surroundings. One of the chief spokesmen for the radical right, for example, had sat in on the class of a French scholar at Harvard, with her permission, and then maliciously misrepresented what had gone on there. Dartmouth, to mention no other college, provided ample evidence of right-wing malice in action. Hardly an encouraging thought. Kate was hoping for a fraternity prank, though kidnapping was serious and they would suffer for it. That she had long since promised herself.

Reminding herself of the waiting Harriet, Kate searched her notes for the addresses of the four resentful students. Not, she realized, that they are necessarily still living there. Students move around a lot, and some of them had given just their parents' address. As she had guessed, none of the four, two men and two women, lived in a college or graduate dormitory.

List of addresses in hand, Kate returned to the living room. "I've a task for you too," she said to Harriet. "Here are four addresses with names. Would you go to the two addresses where the women live and dream up something—you're inspecting for roaches, the university is thinking of combining apartments, whatever. You're better at this than I am. You're so delightfully harmless looking—grandmotherly, not to put too fine a point on it—that I don't think they'd hesitate to let you in if you're both unthreatening and persistent. I want to know the same stuff Toni's finding out: would it be possible for them to be hiding Reed? Don't do anything about it, just investigate and then let me know."

"Right you are," Harriet said, rising to her feet. "Back to the old entrance trick; I've always claimed gray-haired women of sufficient age can get in anywhere and are later unidentifiable. I'll report soon— that is, if Toni hasn't insisted on abandoning you and the case. Oh, hell, I'll let you know what happens, whatever happens. Don't forget to check for messages tomorrow at the vet's, sometime in the afternoon."

And Harriet was gone.

Five

WHEN Kate and Banny went around to their training class the next afternoon—the classes were offered at various hours, and once enrolled, owner and dog might come to the class most convenient to their schedule—there were two messages offered by Ovido. Toni, her annoyance at the flaunting of her orders fairly sizzling off the paper, reported that her assignment was complete, and that she would report to Kate that evening, *not* in Kate's apartment, but above the boat basin on Seventy-ninth Street in Riverside Park, Kate to turn up with dog at seven P.M. Don't look for her; she would spot Kate.

The second message was from Harriet saying she would be at Kate's apartment at six with extraordinary news. It was with some difficulty that Kate kept herself attentive to the lesson and Banny's tendency to wander off and inspect the other dogs. Kate's barely controllable urge to rush home and wait for Harriet was all too clearly apparent to Banny, who kept heading for the exit. It was not one of their better sessions.

Eventually the class was dismissed, not without a frown at Kate (not Banny) from the patient instructor. Kate departed guiltily but immediately, and they ran home—with Kate carrying Banny, who was not prepared to rush at so pell-mell a pace.

Harriet was there.

"Well?" Kate said when they arrived upstairs. She knew Harriet would not have held out the promise of news if there was not news, probably good news, in the offing.

"Sit down," Harriet said. "This is going to take some working out, so don't leap to your feet and rush out the door like a lunatic. Listen. I said sit down."

Kate sat.

"Good," Harriet said. "I understand you're meeting Toni tonight, and she'll tell you her findings and plans. I gather she had a somewhat raunchy time with the fraternity boys and picked up some interesting clues, but nothing decisive. I, on the other hand, have real news. Don't interrupt." Once again Kate subsided.

"The two women on your list lived in quite different circumstances. The first had a small, one-room apartment, hardly room to swing a cat—though I have always been shocked at the idea that anyone would want to swing a cat—all right, all right, and the other lived in a large apartment shared with three other women. Only two of the four were home, including the name on your list. She looked decidedly unwilling to let me into the apartment, or even inside the door, but I did a pretty good act, though I say it myself, of an authoritative person from the university housing office—"

"You mean it was a university apartment?" Kate asked. "I didn't know they gave large apartments to students."

"They don't. It turned out that one of the young women was the granddaughter of a retired professor, more or less illegally occupying his apartment with three roommates to help with the rent. I had a suspicion the university wasn't too happy about this, given the shortage of large apartments, and that made my threats of what might happen if they didn't let me in more convincing. I'd taken the precaution of visiting the housing office first, passing myself off as the dithering aunt of a student, and found out that the apartment house in question was university property. Now don't rush me, Kate, we can't do anything right now, so contain yourself. Whatever that means.

"After I got in, I asked to be shown the whole apartment and to be given a detailed account of who was living there, their university status, the number of people in each room—that sort of thing. And here's the clincher. One of the rooms was locked, and they said they couldn't possibly let me into it because its occupant, presumably a young woman, was ill with the flu and several other feverish and quite contagious ailments. I said I would risk the ailments; please unlock the door. They stubbornly refused, and I made large noises about reporting this to the authorities when the occupant of the room coughed and then began singing, softly but unmistakably, in a baritone voice. What's more, he, or up to that moment the possibility of a very hoarse, deep-voiced woman, was singing 'Loch Lomond.' "

"It was Reed!" Kate screamed, jumping to her feet. "You and he were always going on about that song, how you could never tell whom the singer was talking to, his true love or his friend, and why they were taking different roads."

"I do remember, my dear. We discussed it one whole evening shortly after we all met, at the first mention of single malt Scotch as I recall. We kept sipping and wondering why one was taking the high road and one the low road, and whether the roads were metaphorical or geographical—"

"Harriet, please."

"Well, my dear, they tried to lead me away from the door, but I spoke up and he sang it again. I'm sure he heard me. So that is probably where he is."

"I'd already gathered that," Kate said, beside herself. "Why are we just sitting here? Are you trying to drive me mad? Is this some sort of sadistic practice you and Toni are developing for unknown reasons?"

"When I left the apartment sometime later, not hurrying in my inspection so that they would think I hadn't noticed much—in fact, I had suggested by a certain knowing, disapproving look that I understood that one of the young women had her lover with her in that room—where was I? Oh, yes, I finally made my slow way out of the place, doing my best to calm any suspicions they might have of my interest in the locked room, taking notes and muttering about renting so many rooms and sanitary conditions and everything I could think of. I'm pretty sure I had calmed their fears. But I stopped at a phone on the corner and called Toni. She arranged for some of her operators to stand at the apartment house entrances once I left and make sure they didn't try to move their prisoner."

"Suppose they had?"

"They would have been stopped, of course. Those operators are large men with weapons. Fortunately, nothing happened. The operators are still there, by the way, connected to Toni by cellular phones. You and I will go around to meet Toni at seven as previously scheduled and then we'll go and liberate Reed. He didn't sound at all bad, not in pain or weak or anything, so I don't think there's much to worry about. What time is it now?" Harriet gazed at her watch. "That late?" she exclaimed, in what Kate thought a highly irritating manner. "Perhaps we better get going soon."

"Toni said to bring Banny," Kate said. "But surely,

if we're going to storm that apartment and rescue Reed—"

"We're not going to storm the apartment. We're going to pay a call, three well-dressed ladies complete with puppy. I, as the inspector of the afternoon, will say that my two companions are particularly eager to take over this apartment and may they please look at it. I shall remind them that they are probably there illegally, and it would be better for them if they cooperated. Once in, we'll spring Reed, with Toni in charge, definitely in charge. The two operators will be outside the apartment, available if needed. Banny is to come along, first to give you a reason to be in the park, and second to make our visit look innocent and what it pretends to be. One hardly enters an apartment with evil intent accompanied by a large puppy. Of course, if you'd rather wait for Reed here, you and Banny—"

"We're on our way," Kate said, getting her jacket and Banny's leash. "I'm going to have a word or two or three to say about your high-handedness in this whole matter. Or perhaps I should say Toni's high-handedness." Kate ushered Harriet out, locked the door, and awaited the elevator with unconcealed impatience.

The whole operation of freeing Reed could not qualify for a place in any account of dramatic rescues. Harriet, using the method she'd described to Kate, bullied herself, Toni, Kate, and Banny through the apartment door. All the young women were home. Kate's student recognized her and blanched, although, as they would later discover, her look of horror was merely at seeing her professor under these circumstances; she had not known Kate's connection to the man she and her roommates were imprisoning when she agreed to go along with the scheme.

Harriet immediately began showing the layout in the manner of a real estate agent, flinging open doors and identifying the rooms. When they came to the room where Reed had been heard singing "Loch Lomond," Harriet tried the door and reacted with shocked disbelief to find it locked. "Open this door at once," she imperiously said.

"One of our roommates is sick in there," the renter of the apartment said. "We really can't disturb her. That room is no different than the others."

"*From* the others, please," Harriet insisted. "Let us try to preserve what is left to us of a once proud language. No different it may be, but we want to see it. We will tiptoe in no farther than the entrance to look around." Banny, meanwhile, had jumped up on the door, perhaps feeling it her doggy duty to embody Kate's fervor.

"What a cute puppy," the young woman said, a last diversionary tactic.

"Open the damn door—*now*," Toni ordered. For a moment Kate expected her to flourish a revolver, but she withheld that gesture, if only for a moment.

"Open the door or I'll force it open," she said. She retreated down the hall, clearly readying herself for a run and a lunge to smash the door in. "Stand back, Reed," she shouted. *"Here I come."*

"All right, all right," the young woman said. "Here's the key." And she removed it from her pocket. "I told you this wouldn't work," she said to the three other young women. Glumly, she gave Toni the key. Toni handed it to Kate, who found her hand shaking as she put the key in the lock. Toni retrieved the key, opened the door, and stepped back. Kate moved in and Reed moved out, into each other's arms. Banny leapt up on Reed.

"And who the hell is this?" Reed asked, bending down to seize the puppy. "And where's the brandy? Don't Saint Bernards always have a small cask of brandy around their necks when they rescue people?"

Reed, Kate, and Banny were about to set off for home when Toni appeared with the two operators. Someday I must ask them their names, Kate thought, and stop considering them only by their function.

Toni asked the men to make sure no one left the apartment, and then asked Reed and Kate to sit down a moment and listen to her. "Please," she all but commanded, as they looked reluctant. "Harriet has those young women corralled in a room. She's keeping them away from telephones, and doing her best, which we know will be stunning, to fill them with apprehension. Naturally, she's muttering on about the illegality of this apartment, but I told her, never mind that, just keep them worried.

"I have a proposition," Toni said then, "a plan which I think will be a good, if chancy idea. But it's you two who will have to implement it, so let me outline it and then you can tell me what you think. Here's my plan. So far, no one knows that Reed has been found and liberated, except those four tootsies locked in the room with Harriet. I have no doubt they are getting very nervous and regretting their part in this kidnapping."

"From what I saw of them," Reed interrupted, "I think you are right, except perhaps for the blonde with the short skirt. She seemed almost to be enjoying herself."

"We'll have to watch out for her with special care," Toni responded, while Kate looked at Reed with speculation and concern. "What I should do at this moment is call the police and turn them in on a kidnapping charge. The police will, I think, certainly with your lawyerly help"—she nodded at Reed—"persuade the girls to turn state's evidence, that is, to gain immunity in exchange for ratting on the others—that is, the boys. That would be a very useful thing to do, and I certainly would like to nab those boys and scare the shit out of them. However, there's another way." She paused, making certain she had the attention of her listeners.

"This would be a lot harder on you two," she said, "and whether or not we do it depends on how eager you are to catch, not the boys and girls, but the grownups and the organization, if any, behind all this. I don't think the boys originated this plan, but I could be mistaken. Reed, Kate had a theory involving disaffected students of hers, and she was certainly right up to a point. But I think those students were simply instruments of a larger and more dangerous purpose."

"I'm inclined to agree," Reed said.

"Good." Toni looked at Kate. "What I suggest is this: we don't rescue Reed publicly. We don't call the police. We hold the girls for a time, let Kate write the article the kidnappers demanded—let me get this whole plan out," she insisted, as Kate started to object, "and keep the girls happy while, at least for a few days, we try to root out the adult manipulators."

"I won't write an article saying I've repudiated feminism and joined the Christian right, and that's final," Kate said with some asperity.

"I agree with her," Reed said. "Even if we later set forth all the reasons for her having done it, the harm would be done."

"All right, all right," Toni said. "I won't argue the point. But let's say that Kate writes something—what is yet to be decided. Will you go along with the rest of the plan?"

Reed and Kate looked at each other. "I'm sorry you haven't more time to consider," Toni said, "but if I'm going to call the police I have to decide that soon. Delays are hard to explain."

Reed took Kate's hand. "Let's say we won't call them, if Kate agrees. What next, or haven't you got that far? And do Kate and I just camp out here?"

"I thought you might have a friend you can impose on," Toni said. "Preferably one without any doormen or lobby attendants."

"There's Leslie," Kate said. "She lives in a loft. It's just a matter of pressing buttons and then having them send the elevator down. Of course, there's always the chance of someone else in the building coming in or out."

"We'll have to risk that. Can you call her?"

Kate looked at Reed, who nodded. "All right," Kate said, walking over to the phone. The telephone conversation was short. Leslie, being an old and true friend, had simply said, if you're in trouble, come and stay. I'll give you the bedroom.

"Which," Kate explained to Reed on the way down there in Toni's car, "means that they are giving us the only enclosed room in the loft. They'll sleep on a futon in the living room. Very good of them. There's privacy as to sight, though not a lot as to sound, if you see what I mean."

"We'll whisper," he said, consoling her.

But when they arrived, Leslie and Jane, having welcomed them, exclaimed suitably over Banny asleep in Reed's arms, and asked if there was anything they needed, announced they were going out for the evening. "Previous engagement," Jane said, before their protests reached expression. "A friend is doing a gig and we'll stay for the party afterward. Help yourself to anything you want. We'll satisfy our curiosity in the morning." Leslie hugged Kate again, and they left.

Reed pointed to a bottle of Scotch prominently offered on the kitchen counter.

"Would you rather have a brandy?" Kate asked.

"Well, surely it's never too early to begin to train her to bring brandy, though she does look rather young," Reed remarked. He put Banny down on the couch beside Kate, and went for the Scotch. "How old is she? Where did you get her, and is she to be part of the family? As to your question, Scotch would be fine." He poured some for himself and Kate. "Is there something for Banny?"

Poor Banny, Kate thought, destined to be our only topic of conversation. "She isn't ours to keep," Kate said as they returned to what Kate called the living room, although it was only a section of the loft with living room furniture. "She's on loan, as the excuse for undetected messages. I'll explain it all sometime. You talk, Reed. Tell me what happened. Are you really all right?"

"I think we should keep her as our mascot. She'll give us an excuse to meet in the park and exchange kisses. All right, yes, I'm all right. I got nabbed, was kept for a day or two in the smelly room of one of the guys who nabbed me, and then I was moved to the place where you found me. It was only a matter of a few days, though it seemed like forever."

"It seemed that way to me too. Were they mean to you?"

They sipped their Scotch. To Kate's discomfort, conversation between her and Reed, which had not seemed possible in Toni's presence, was still a bit stilted, awkward, not at all what she had supposed it would be when finally—or *if*, as for a time she had thought—they met.

"Not mean." Reed contemplated his glass, emptied it, and then took Kate's hand. "Just seductive," he said, "continually, and more and more persuasively. That was after we got to the girls' apartment, of course."

"What did they want to seduce you to do?"

"Screw them. As acrobatically as possible, I assumed." Reed took a large swallow of Scotch and got up to fetch more. He took Kate's glass too.

"Did you resist," Kate asked, "and if so, why, and if not, why not?" She realized that her tone did not achieve quite the quality of playful indifference for which she had aimed.

Reed answered flatly enough. "Good question. I'd like to say it was out of determined fidelity to you, despite the temptations and their temporary nature, but the truth my darling is that if a fuck would have got me out of there, I would have been more than willing, even without the flaunted lusciousness of the seducers. The last nymph, the blonde, half naked and alluring, did her best. I suggested that we repair to a hotel where we could enjoy ourselves in guaranteed isolation. When she declined that, I knew I'd been right."

"Right about what? Am I being particularly stupid?"

"No, just insufficiently male. I'd suspected from the beginning that what they wanted were photographs, video, and stills. Think what they could have done with them. 'Feminist's husband finds relief at last,' or whatever nastiness they, with the eager help of the media, might have made public. Not to mention that such pictures would not do my career any particular good, whatever delight they might have given the majority of my colleagues. They went on about wanting mature men like me, blah, blah, but when the blonde refused the hotel, I knew they had to stay where the cameras were operating. I do hope Harriet looks for them."

"Hadn't we better let her know?"

"I daresay she and Toni will have thought of searching the place. They were clever to figure out where I'd be."

"I figured it out," Kate said, with a degree of insistence that surprised her. "Not that they didn't do good work. Oh, damn."

"Please don't cry, Kate, that is a quite unsuitable response to my return. Finish your drink. Tell me about every moment you spent since I failed to show up at that restaurant. Because Toni is right. We've got to get our wits working. We've got to figure out, starting tomorrow, who was behind all this. Sure, it was boyish and girlish pranks, but they didn't invent it, and they didn't work out the details. They told me that I would be kept until you wrote an article saying you were no longer a feminist but were embracing all the family values of the Christian right. I said no one would believe it, but they said you had only a short time in which to comply. I hope like hell you didn't."

"I didn't, but I would have if we hadn't found you. And I can't stop crying. Did you really want to screw those girls?"

"Passionately. Have you ever heard the phrase *to fuck somebody*, as in 'He really fucked me over, man?' I would have enjoyed fucking them over nine ways to Christmas. But I didn't. Kate, what's happened to your sense of humor?"

"I think I've lost it," Kate said.

"No you haven't," Reed said. "Never, never. It must have been horrible for you. I was just locked up, fed regularly, and shown a parade of seductive young things. You were sick with worry. If you want to really laugh, try to think of our positions reversed."

"It's not the same thing," Kate said.

"No," Reed said, "it's not. It was a mean and horrible thing to do to you, and I have every intention of finding the people behind this and making them pay. It's not any different, except in degree, from fundamentalist violence everywhere. If people don't see things their way, they deserve to suffer. I knew this country had become vulnerable to terrorists, and now I know it personally. So do you. Shall we get

73

really drunk? I wish we could switch to champagne, however inadvisable that would be, but we're lucky to have what we do. You have good friends, Kate."

And at last she smiled.

Six

THE next morning four of them, Kate and Reed and Toni and Leslie, held a council of war in Leslie's loft. Harriet was guarding the "girls," as Toni and Reed continued to call them. Jane, who—as Leslie the artist liked to put it—worked for a living, had left earlier. She was in their confidence but was not able to be part of their consultation. Leslie, who had been brought up to date on the events and discussions of the previous evening, announced her agreement with Toni's plan.

"You two can stay here as long as you like," she said to Reed and Kate. "After grandchildren, believe me, you will hardly be noticed." But of course they would be. Lofts are designed for one or two people, never more, not unless one built a lot of rooms—in which case why not rent an ordinary apartment? Leslie and Jane had raised the bedroom walls to assure themselves of privacy in case of guests, but otherwise it was all open space.

"That's generous of you and Jane," Toni said, "but I think it will make most sense to let Kate and Reed go home. Kate can go home in the ordinary way. We'll have to sneak Reed in, wrapped in a Persian rug like Cleopatra if necessary. He'll have to pretend not to be there with Kate, which, once he's in, shouldn't be too hard. But what about your teaching?" she asked Reed.

"If I'm kidnapped, I can't teach. I've already missed classes. It's true that when they learn that I could have returned and didn't there'll be a certain amount of explaining to do, but I think I can straighten it all out and make it up to the students. The question is, once Kate and I are returned home, what next?"

"Let's get you home first," Toni said. And by providing suitable diversions for the doorman and arranging for the fire stair to be opened for Reed's ascent (the elevator being closely monitored), getting him in the apartment was accomplished without too much difficulty. Toni, Kate was mildly amused to observe, went into her sexy act to distract the doorman while she, Kate, having returned to the apartment in the elevator, descended the stairway to the ground floor and from inside released the gate for Reed and Toni, who by that time had persuaded the doorman to look around the corner to see if her car was likely to be ticketed. It was all a matter of a few moments. The doorman, having earlier been memorably greeted by Kate, was prepared to swear that she had returned to the apartment alone with the cute puppy.

The three of them, once home, and after Reed had changed his clothes, settled down to continue their council.

Toni began. "With the girls held in their apartment incommunicado—that's going to be Harriet's job, dealing with the phone, visitors, whatever comes up—everyone but those girls will assume Reed is still properly kidnapped. Either the powers that be, the ones we're searching for, will get in touch with the girls about Reed or they won't. If they don't, fine. If they do, we have to have a plan. The point is, you see, that with Kate willing to write her article, they have every reason to wait patiently."

"But surely they're going to want a report from the girls."

"Surely, and with Harriet's threats the girls, or the one she selects, will tell them what we want them to hear. This can't go on for very long, as you can see, so I suggest that Kate send in her article today or tomorrow."

"Saying what exactly?" Kate asked.

"I've been thinking about that," Reed said. "If you don't send in an article, they'll threaten to do something terrible to me, but since I'm here, they can hardly do it. They would then, of course, find out I wasn't where they thought I was. If you do send in

77

the article it will come to exactly the same thing in the end, since the article, however cleverly you devise it, will not be what they want. So"—here he turned to Toni—"why should Kate bother writing?"

"Here's my reasoning," Toni said. "They're planning to run the article in one of their right-wing journals or papers, so you know that what you write will be printed. Why not write something in code, like every other word says what you mean while the whole reads as though you were saying what they wanted? Then, when the article is picked up by the media, you can tell the whole story. And the code will indicate that you haven't really done what they wanted but rather the opposite."

"Where will that get us?" Kate asked.

"Probably nowhere. But it will give us a short time in which to trap them before they discover that Reed has eluded them. In that short time, we'll try to set up a case of kidnapping and blackmail against the bastards. If you don't send in the article in a day or so they'll take immediate action of some sort and discover that Reed's gone, and we'll have lost the testimony of the girls, who when that happens will have every reason to deny their part in the kidnapping."

"You overestimate me," Kate said. "I've never been any good at word games or codes, much as I admire those people who can break them. But I know what I'll do. When I was visiting Radcliffe many years ago, a young man gave a graduation speech that the whole audience applauded, all about law and order, getting

78

crime off the streets, that sort of thing, and when they had finished their wild expressions of appreciation, he told them his words had been written by Hitler. I'll bet I can find a passage from Hitler that they will accept as my perfect renunciation of all women's rights. Later, I'll identify the author."

"Sounds okay—if you think they'll go for it. I suspect they will."

"The first thing Hitler was against was women outside the home. Family values, provided the family was Aryan, were his ideal. He didn't get around to killing the Jews till later."

"The things you know," Toni said. "Well, I'm off. Reed, do take care not to be seen by anyone like a delivery man, or the man on the back elevator, or someone cleaning the hall—you know."

"I'll be careful," Reed said.

"I know, I know." Toni smirked at him. "You think, and Kate thinks, and Harriet certainly thinks, that I'm too bossy and too eager to take charge. But I get things done, and I figure results are better than smooth manners. If you disagree, I'm always dischargeable."

"We'll take it under advisement," Reed said, smiling. "While Kate's searching out the perfect passage from Hitler, don't forget to let us know what the next step is."

"Check your e-mail," Toni said. "I'll be back."

"I thought you thought they were keeping a watch on me," Kate said.

"So they probably are. But with Leslie visiting and

maybe Jane and Harriet, they can't keep track of everybody. And do remember, dear Kate, we are no longer worried about Reed's safety."

And with that, she swept from the room and the apartment.

"Bossy but probably effective," Reed said.

"I'm holding my opinion in abeyance," Kate responded. "Must I rush off and contemplate the writings of Adolf Hitler?"

"Not immediately," Reed said. "We'll both work on it in a little while. Right now, I could use a bit of a nap. Where does Banny sleep, by the way?"

"In our bed, I'm afraid. She was a comfort."

"Are we keeping her?"

"We can't, Reed. That was made very clear. She's a dog with outstanding conformation, apparently evident at her birth. She's wanted by her owners, for breeding and I hope love."

"We'll keep her for now. We may need her for more messages. Do you think she can manage to sleep in the kitchen if we shut the door?"

"Absolutely not," Kate said. "Under the bed is the most we can hope for."

"Well," Reed said, "she'll be a nice change from incarceration by nymphs. You'd be a nice change too." And Banny, pleased with that, jumped up on the couch and licked his face.

Kate woke after their somewhat extended nap and stayed quiet, pondering their situation but not wanting to wake Reed, when a slight stirring in the bed revealed Banny sleeping at his feet.

"I'm awake," he said. "I know she shouldn't be up here, but I thought, with a total lack of consideration, it will be the problem of the lady who will have to bring her up. I am merely an indulgent foster parent."

"How are you?" Kate asked.

"Dissatisfied with the current plan; I've been mulling it over. How about you?"

"Very dissatisfied. I began to realize, rather belatedly after they had kidnapped you, that I was being wholly passive in the plan for your retrieval. I suppose the shock was so great it took me a while to wake up. I feel that we're being pushed into something of the same position again. I'm rather sure I don't like it. Not that Toni and Harriet don't mean well."

"They mean the best. And from a certain point of view, their plan is a sensible one. The only trouble is, it doesn't sit well with me. I don't like hiding out, I don't like your being the only target—nor would you like me to be—and I think that the more people we involve in this caper, the more successful we will be. Finding out who kidnapped me, who was behind it, isn't the hard part. It's what sort of support and organization is behind *them*. Do you agree?"

"Totally," Kate said. "I'm relieved, because I didn't like the thought of urging you back into the open where you could be assaulted again. On the other hand, I want to be out there, talking about this, asking for help, finding out where everybody stands. You know it's a risk, though, beyond the personal risk of danger to us. We may, we almost certainly will, get tarred with the brush of left radicalism. My thought is, it's time someone was willing to say what he or she believes."

"Yes. We walk in fear, while the radical right trumpets its lies and delusions. Someone has to do something."

"True." Kate reached over to touch him. Banny crawled farther up the bed until she was completely between them, making Kate laugh. "Who knows what your law school and my English department, let alone my university, will say about all this, but hell, what is tenure for? I shall never stop worrying about you, however, and that troubles me. I was shocked at how profound the shock was, if you see what I mean—the shock of your being simply lifted like that, taken from our daily life."

"Indicating a weakness?"

"Indicating a dependency. Frightening, that, and don't laugh."

"I wouldn't dream of laughing. And if I felt equally or even more desperately shocked by your being kidnapped, that would just be normal male behavior: a man doesn't want others messing around with his woman. Is that it?"

"Fair enough. We all know about men; they are desperate for a while, and then find another wife, or female companion, whatever. I felt what I felt was different, frighteningly different. I was scared, not to put too fine a point on it."

"Yes," Reed said. "It's always hard to discover one's vulnerability. Particularly when one had declared oneself satisfactorily unassailable."

"That's nonsense." Their hands met, brushing down Banny's coat. "Who knows better than you how assailed I've been. You might even say that being assailed was my way of being. But to be paralyzed as I was, to be stricken into such passivity, that was terrifying."

"Yes, I see. I do see. Well, no more paralysis, no more passivity. What do we tell Harriet and Toni? That I, having been rescued, will take over the operation in partnership with you?"

"We certainly have to talk to them. Let's call and request a meeting. I think we'd better get Harriet to call Banny's owner too. We're getting too intimate with a dog we can't keep. Anyway, how could we keep a dog while pursuing the radical right?"

"Point well taken," Reed said, ruffling the dog's hair. "Call Harriet now."

Toni and Harriet, having been tracked down through beepers and other electronic beckoning devices, gathered at Kate and Reed's apartment in the late afternoon. Drinks were offered. Toni refused, suggesting, only half humorously, that Harriet drank enough for the two of them, but Kate suspected that Toni never drank at work and, if she drank at all, did so only at home, off the job—an admirable policy but considerably out of line with the image of American private eyes. Still, Kate thought, almost everything these days is out of line with our images. Some of us want to revive the old forms, and others, like Reed and me, want to move on.

Kate and Reed had agreed that he would speak first, partly because he was the one supposed to be hiding out, and partly because he wasn't the one who had hired them and could therefore criticize their plan with less offense, or so he hoped.

"Kate and I," he began, "want to offer a different plan of action. We've talked this over, and we both feel strongly that we should get back to our jobs, and speak publicly about what has happened and about our eagerness to discover the contrivers of the plot—not the students, but those who planned the students' moves and thought up the whole scheme. This doesn't mean that we don't want you to continue working with us, if you will agree to. It does mean that everything we do is proposed in consultation and agreed upon by us all. We'd like you to continue underground, as it were, while Kate and I operate in the open. How does that strike you?"

"What about the girls still being held in that apartment? Harriet left them with my operators when she came here at your urgent request," Toni said, in a tone of voice indicating her disapproval of this development.

"I think we shall have to turn them over to the police now," Reed said. "I know you've left yourself open to severe complaints, at the least for not calling the police at once, and I intend to take the blame for that. No, nothing noble," he said as Toni began to object. "It might well have been a logical request of mine at the time, and I think I'll be able to deal with the consequences a lot more easily than you. For one thing, I've got connections left over from my days in the D.A.'s office, and for another, I'm less vulnerable, not being a private eye, always a suspicious identity to the police. Why don't you call your operators and then call the police now?"

"That means the girls may not talk," Toni said.

"I think they probably will." Reed looked at his hands. "After all, I'm a valid witness; they may well want to cut their losses. And I don't think those girls know who was behind all this, other than Kate's student's boyfriend who bullied or persuaded them into it."

"All right," Toni said. "I'll call. But I'm by no means going along with the rest of this until I hear a lot more about it." She went into the hall to use the telephone.

"And when she's finished," Kate said to Harriet, "maybe you could call and tell the breeder who owns Banny to take her back. We don't need an excuse for messages anymore, and we're getting too attached to her, not to mention teaching her bad habits."

"What bad habits?" Harriet asked, intrigued.

"Never mind. Just call. Either the breeder can pick her up, or we'll manage to deliver her, though I'd rather it were a quicker parting than that. She's a very appealing little bugger."

Toni returned and Harriet went to use the hall phone. While she was gone, Toni, who clearly had something on her mind, decided to get it off. "I've felt from the start," she said to Kate, "that you didn't really trust or like me, and that it was only because of Harriet that you even considered hiring me professionally. That being the case, maybe we'd better part now. We can just consider the job we were hired for over; Reed is back, and the people holding him are in custody."

Reed looked at Kate: your move, he indicated. Kate was about to speak when Harriet returned. "The woman who lent us Banny can't come for her any day soon because her kennel person is ill and she can't leave the place long enough to drive to New York City. But she has heard from Dorothy Hedge, who turns out to be a neighbor—that is, much closer than New York City, though some miles nearer New York than the breeder, whose name is Marjorie—that you were there, that is, visiting Dorothy Hedge. I'm afraid I completely lost control of that sentence, but maybe its meaning has seeped through. This all came about because Dorothy Hedge knew that Marjorie bred Saint Bernards and called to ask about Banny. I'm not altogether sure she didn't slightly suspect you may have stolen the dog, but that point was passed over rather lightly. Marjorie explained lending Banny, and asked Dorothy to receive her when you're able to deliver. Is that, if far from perfectly clear, acceptable?"

"It's odd," Kate said, "but I'm not sure why. I had hoped to simply hand Banny over, but I'll drive her up there tomorrow if that's all right with Dorothy Hedge. Oh, lord, I'd almost forgotten that I promised to see her again on Thursday to learn more about her family. Well, this visit will have to serve instead. But I shan't like saying goodbye to Banny."

"I'll go with you," Reed said. "Of course I will."

"Nice thought. But you'd better get back to your teaching or they'll think you're taking the whole semester off."

"I'll show up in the morning and we'll drive up with Banny in the afternoon. That's settled. Agreed?"

"Agreed," said Kate, who was relieved. Harriet said she would call Marjorie back now to tell her to tell Dorothy to expect Kate and Reed.

"And then," Toni said, "perhaps we can at least get an outline of your plan, and our part in it, if any."

"That's simple," Kate said, "if you'll agree. Reed and I will do our best to stir things up. If there are any leads, or ideas, we'd very much like you to follow them. While we will be out there collecting the slings and arrows of outrageous fortune, you will be less obviously involved and able to make inquiries and follow leads. Sorry about my weak and repetitive vocabulary but I seem to have only the most conventional set of words at hand when it comes to what private eyes do."

Toni smiled and seemed, almost perceptibly, to relax. "It's okay with me, I guess. It's a job, and we're not exactly raking in the fees at the moment; so fine, you're on. You tell us what to do and we'll do it. Harriet can go on being the invisible old lady who can get in anywhere, and I'll go on being the sexpot who uses the magician's trick of making you watch one hand while the necessary business is accomplished by the other. If it's all right with Harriet, that is."

"It's fine with me," Harriet said, returning in time to catch the gist. "Dorothy expects both of you plus puppy dog tomorrow afternoon, anytime. She is used to the trauma of parting, and will give what help she can. So that's done."

"I guess that's enough for today. Do you think so, Kate?"

"I think so. Shall we all have another drink?"

"We'll leave you three to your last evening together," Harriet said in tones of profound drama. "Come on, Toni. We're only wanted once the bullets begin to fly. A metaphor," she quickly added, catching Reed's eye. And taking Toni by the arm, she extracted them both from the apartment with amazing efficiency.

"I thought she'd at least have another drink, a farewell to Banny," Kate said. "It's not like Harriet."

"I think she felt we needed to be alone."

"Well," Kate said, "I think she was right. But there's no food in the house, except puppy chow for Banny. I kind of let things drop."

"There's always Chinese takeout and the telephone," Reed said. "Like Woody Allen in his movies, we can eat it in bed out of the cartons and watch television."

"Nothing on television," Kate said.

"I know," Reed said. "There never is."

Seven

ARLY the next day Kate and Reed held a conference over their coffee, an unusual gambit, since Reed's classes were earlier than Kate's and he always left while she was still asleep. Today they had both risen early to review their new plan of action.

"We are not only going to be in the open, in a way hardly familiar to either of us," Reed said, "but we must go out of our way to recount the adventures of the last few days to anyone we meet. That will be easier for me, since I will have, in any case, to explain my absence. But you must do your best, going on about how worried you were, making clear that you and the article you would have been forced to write were the real object of the exercise."

"Do you intend to describe the sexual details of your incarceration?"

"No. I know it's no good telling you to forget that, but it's hardly the most important detail in all this. Do try to remember, dear Kate, that I may have been snatched, but you were the target. Eventually, of course, when we both decide the moment has come, I'll go into all the gory details."

"The point, I gather, is to let as many people as possible know about what happened, pleading the while for any information about who might have been responsible."

"Exactly. We may be wrong, but we have decided that the wider the net, the better the chance of catching something. I don't know if that holds as a fact about deep sea fishing, but it's worth a try in these circumstances. I'll meet you back here to deliver Banny to the Hedge woman. My God, what is to become of Banny this morning?"

"I've thought about it," Kate said, "and I think she'd better stay here, in the kitchen with paper, food, and water—and with the radio playing in the hope that that will console her for her solitude. I did think about taking her with me to the office, but I wasn't up to explaining her, especially since she won't be with us after today."

"Suppose she howls?"

"I know. I worried about that; unfair to the neighbors. But it's only for one day, and if they are home during the day and complain, we'll apologize and say, with perfect veracity, that it will never happen again."

"I'm glad to see you've thought of everything."

"I try," Kate said modestly, with downcast eyes. Reed laughed his appreciation.

"Did I say how good it is to be back?"

"Not in the last hour," Kate said.

When Kate reached her office it was borne in upon her how much harder her task was than Reed's. He, having to explain his absence, had an opening for his revelations; Kate had to create her own openings. It was odd how difficult it was suddenly to say to a class—for they had decided she would say this to her classes today, since they were seminars and not the large lecture—"If I have seemed distracted these past days, please forgive me; you see, they kidnapped my husband and I was worried about him."

She had hoped that someone would exclaim "Kidnapped!" in astonished tones, and she would launch into her story. In the first seminar, however, her students simply stared at her openmouthed, and she had to go on talking for quite a while before she elicited any response at all. But when the response finally came, it was satisfactorily one of outrage, if nonverbal outrage. Kate emphasized the point of the whole scheme's having come from the right, as was evident from the demand for the article and the kidnappers' condemnation of her politics. At this, the seminar's members glanced knowingly at one another, but continued to offer no suggestions or information.

"If," Kate said, into the silence, "any of you knows anything, anything at all, about radical right groups, organizations, or outspoken individuals on this campus, I do ask you to talk to me about them. Either make an appointment with me or come to my office hour, or write me a note on paper or e-mail. Or if you leave a message on my voice mail, I'll return your call. This sort of violence is dangerous, and I do hope that you will help me to discover who is in back of it. I have suffered a good deal, as has my husband, and I want to be sure that neither I nor anyone else has to endure that again. And this is to say nothing of the danger to the university itself." She then, after a significant pause, launched into the subject of the day.

Kate expected her second seminar, scheduled an hour after the first had finished, to be a repeat, but the student and faculty grapevine had already heated up. Kate had dropped into the department office and told her story to the secretarial staff there, as well as to any of her colleagues who happened in. Thus, by the second seminar, she had hardly begun to speak of Reed's kidnapping when she was besieged by questions, suggestions, and warnings. The literary subject of the day abandoned, these students were eager to discuss the political situation at the university.

It took Kate but a moment to realize that the first seminar had been for graduate students, who were notoriously cautious; their dependence on the faculty

for recommendations, grades, fellowships, and ultimately jobs was great enough to discourage offending anyone in power. This seminar, an undergraduate
one, was encumbered by no such trepidations. These
college students were more than ready to give their
views on anything and everything, particularly if in
doing so they could avoid too detailed a discussion of
the assignment, which had been long and of an ar-
duous nature.

"There's an amazing number of right-wing nuts,"
one young man said.

"Meaning what, exactly?" Kate interrupted. She
needed to have the *nuts* defined. The more exact the
discussion, the more likely it was to lead somewhere.

"They think gun control is a way to disarm citizens
so that the government can take over their land."

"And," a young woman added, "they think women
are their property, and that women's bodies belong to
them."

"They haven't the sense to see that gun control is
only about concealed weapons, and that they can
keep their hunting stuff. Of course, they're also against
banning assault rifles; same reason as before."

Descriptions of the right-wing ideas that were
sweeping the campus—in the view of these students—
continued for a while. With a shock Kate realized
that no undergraduate with right-wing sympathies
would have taken her class except, in the manner of
some of the right-wing phalanx at Dartmouth, to spy
on it. What she had here, it seemed, was a bunch of

liberal, feminist environmentalists, probably in favor of welfare, national health care, and food for hungry families with children. Without question, these were the sort who were interested not only in literature but in the questions they might ask of it. And because of the time in which they were living, those questions inevitably touched on race, class, gender, and sexual orientation—subjects anathema to the right. For the first time it came home to Kate that she was already politically tagged, and that that tag was well known to all undergraduate students and probably a fair proportion of the faculty. This was, somehow, a slightly shocking revelation—it is always disturbing to discover we have been labeled—but it at least made her investigation in some ways easier.

With the conclusion of her undergraduate seminar, Kate made her way to her office in preparation for meeting Reed and (or primarily, as she hardly admitted to herself) for rescuing poor, deserted Banny. A young man was waiting for her outside her office door.

"I might be some help in your search for the kidnappers," he said.

"Come in." Kate opened the door, beckoning to him. "I haven't much time at the moment, but let's introduce ourselves anyway."

"My name is Morton Weldon," he said, offering his hand, which Kate shook. "I know your name. I won't take long now." Seating himself, he reached into his backpack and extracted a piece of paper. "This may help some; I hope so." He handed Kate the paper.

Glancing at it, she saw it was a list, with campus addresses.

"I'm gay," Mr. Weldon said. "Out-of-the-closet gay. No earring, but determination. I've had a lot of very nasty letters, disgusting signs in my room and on my door after I locked it, and not too long ago, a letter with a bullet in it and a note saying it should be in me."

Kate's horror must have shown on her face.

"Yes, it's interesting what the administration decides not to look into. There are acceptable targets of everything this side of actual physical violence and then there are unacceptable targets. Maybe we can talk about it sometime. I got mad enough at all this to get together a list of the worst homophobes. Of course, anyone who was acting alone and in secret wouldn't be on my list. But in my opinion, college bigots rarely act alone or in secret. So I thought there might be a connection between the homophobes and the right-wing kidnappers. Anyway, check it out." And, zippering up his backpack, he rose to go.

"Thank you," Kate said. "I hope we can talk again when I am not in a hurry. Will you make an appointment or come back in an office hour?"

"Sure. My name's on the list there, with my number, so you can call too if you want some clarification. Ciao."

"By the way," Kate said, stopping him at the door, "how did you hear about all this so fast? You're not in any of my classes."

"No. But a good friend of mine is one of your graduate students. Admires you, too. So I thought I'd stop in and do what I could. Ciao again."

Stunned for a moment, Kate at last gathered up her belongings to head homeward. In the hall she encountered a male colleague.

"I know, you're leaving," he said, glancing at Kate's briefcase. "I just wanted to tell you about a friend of mine who teaches religion in the Midwest. She's prominent in her field, and gives the large introductory lecture course on the history of Christianity—mostly freshmen. The students fill out teacher evaluations. You should have seen some of the evaluations from the Christian right. They gave her zero, and wrote things like 'blasphemer'; 'She only spent a week on Jesus' life'; 'She doesn't think the Bible is God's truth,' and so on. This is in one of the country's outstanding universities. I just thought I'd pass it on. I guess we should have known since Oklahoma City that the right, and particularly the militia on the right, are not a bunch of law-abiding dissenters, but I think it's getting just a little bit hairy, don't you? Kidnapping, I ask you!" And he hurried down the hall, not unlike, Kate thought, Alice's rabbit in happier times.

Reed, having picked up the car at the garage, met Kate at home, where she awaited him in front of their building. The doorman opened the car door for her, and, clinging to Banny, she joined Reed. As he drove away in a great swooping and illegal U-turn, she stroked Banny.

"There is no way we can keep her," Reed said. "No way."

"I know." Kate stroked the puppy, who was settling down in her lap. "Harriet left a letter for me with the doorman; it says, 'To be read en route.' Shall I begin now?"

"Every word from Harriet is to be treasured," Reed said.

"Dear Kate and Reed," Kate read aloud. "While you have been spreading the news of the recent exciting events in your life, I have not deserted the trail. Upon leaving you yesterday evening, I sought out the mother of Dorothy Hedge and that naughty letter-writing student. It turns out that the woman is here from Georgia, where she normally resides, and is visiting her son. I had to betray my deepest convictions and return to the role of spy, the role you, dear Kate, found so unsympathetic. I expressed opinions I would die rather than embrace, but I did it rather well, not overdoing it, just sounding right-wing, weepy (so much more convincing than emphatic rhetoric), and determined to get my own back on the filthy liberals who had ruined our country. I told her I was related to one of the dead at Waco. I had a story ready should she demand it, but she didn't. She seemed relieved to have met someone in New York who thought as she did. Despite the few right-wing, homophobic students,

I can't believe she found many converts here; it must, at any rate, be uphill work."

Kate paused, as Reed had reached the tollbooth on the Henry Hudson Bridge. Banny stirred as the car stopped. Kate soothed her while they waited on line to pay the toll, and resumed her reading of the letter when they were again under way.

"Harriet ought to take up the writing of fiction," Reed said. "Do go on; she's every bit as good as John Grisham."

"I didn't know you read him," Kate said.

"Someone left one of his novels in my office. Well, all lawyers are intrigued by this sort of thing, at least at first. Who doesn't dream of the chance to make millions by putting his litigation experiences into a book? Go on with the letter."

Kate, grinning, continued to read: "She told me that she was particularly grateful to have an older woman to help her. Through her son, she was trying to recruit college students, but she seemed to sense that their devotion was likely to be ephemeral, and she wanted some surer workers in the community. She then told me about stalking abortion clinics in the city; I'll spare you the gruesome details, but it came down to the fact that New York women, joining arms in a kind of barricade, prevented interference with women approaching the clinic. I badly wanted to point out that not all or even most of the women coming to what she insisted on calling 'abortion clinics' were coming to the clinics for abortions, but one does have to remember one's role.

"I'll save further tidbits of our enlightening exchange until we meet over some sustaining libation. For now, I'm suggesting you read this letter en route to Dorothy Hedge because, when I asked her if the son was her only child, she was quite forthcoming about Dorothy, about how Dorothy had betrayed the cause and so on, which was what I wanted to hear. But then, she said something that made me prick up my ears. She mentioned the kennel Dorothy runs, and something about the way she put it convinced me that she had been there. It was a slip, and I pretended not to notice. But if they are such enemies, why did she go to see her at her kennel? Well, there are many possible reasons that do not indicate Dorothy's sympathies with Mama, but I thought I would mention it just so you take care of what you say. Don't reveal anything about Toni or me, or any plans. My suggestion—and I know how little open you and Reed are to suggestions—is to play it kind of dumb. I don't mean that you and Reed could ever appear really dumb. But just say, 'It was such a fright,' and 'I'm so grateful to have Reed back,' and don't go into any details about anything. I know that you, Kate, had decided to trust her, and your instincts may well have been right. But let's be more certain before you trust her anymore. Yours in the fight for the good and true, Harriet."

"Good letter," Reed said. "I think she's suggesting,

without quite daring to say it, that we gush on giddily, and I think she's right."

"Can we possibly be convincing as giddy innocents?"

"We can give it a try. I, for one, have never been kidnapped before. You, for another, have never received a ransom note. I think if we confine ourselves to being a little repetitive about these things, we'll persuade her, at the same time making believable the fact that we've been talking about our adventures to everyone in sight, which, if she is in Mama's confidence, she will know."

As they turned into Dorothy Hedge's driveway to the welcoming chorus of barking dogs, Banny roused herself. Kate opened the car door and let Banny run out toward Dorothy, who was coming from the house to meet them. To Kate's delight, Banny ran back from Dorothy to her and Reed. Kate swooped the puppy up again, and introduced Reed to Dorothy, who shook his hand and congratulated him on his freedom.

"I know it will be hard to give this little rascal up," Dorothy said, asking no further questions at the moment. "But you did tell me you weren't really in a position to have a dog in the city." Dorothy, Kate was amused to notice, considered keeping a dog in the city comparable to keeping a child in a coal cellar. "Well, come into the kitchen and have a cup of tea."

She turned toward the kitchen door and Reed and Kate exchanged a glance that meant: she wants to see what we think and what we plan to do. Their glance confirmed their plan to follow Harriet's suggestion, and Kate launched into her part as soon as they were seated and Dorothy had put the kettle on.

"Yes, as you see," Kate said, attempting to sound breathless, "Reed is back and I can return to my former life with all its blessed calmness." And she reached out to take Reed's hand, thinking, I'll be trying out for the Actors Studio next. Then, after a time, she said, "Thank you." This for the tea when Dorothy had finally made it; they had remained silent until then, watching the preparation of tea, the pouring of tea into the cups, the slicing of a cake. "What I'm really worried about at the moment," Kate added, "is Banny. Not for her sake, but for mine. I shall miss her."

"Of course you will," Dorothy said soothingly. Banny slept at their feet. "Perhaps one day you'll decide to adopt a puppy, perhaps when you stop working and your life becomes more settled. Or perhaps after you have a child."

Kate did not exactly look her age, but that any woman might think her capable of childbearing was shocking. Apparently Dorothy realized this. "I'm afraid that sounded like a stupid remark," she said. "It was a stupid remark, and a conventional one at that. Please let me explain. I've seen so many people acquire dogs as substitutes for children. Often they then have a child, and the dog may suffer. I can't say I approve. But, of course, that is hardly your case. I'm afraid I sometimes go off into one of my speeches without thinking about whom I'm addressing. Do forgive me."

Kate avoided looking at Reed. Dorothy's explanation of her inane remark had a certain cogency, considering her devotion to the canine species; it was, at the same time, unclear whether her first statement or her last reflected her true feelings. And how did those feelings mesh with what she had earlier told Kate?

Reed put down his cup, and stood up; Banny leaped up against his legs. "I think we'd better go," he said. "It will be easier for all of us, but especially for Kate, who has known Banny longest, and of course for Banny herself, if we take a rather swift departure."

Kate too rose to her feet. Dorothy lifted the puppy up, and held her. "You go ahead then," she said. "I'll keep Banny here until she's called for. And try not to worry about her. She'll have a lovely life living with Marjorie as her very own pet dog, and being trained for dog shows. You haven't a thing to worry about. Banny is a beautiful animal; yes she is. Say goodbye, Banny."

Kate and Reed, leaving by the kitchen door, could hear the puppy yelping her protests. They got hastily into the car. "You drive," Reed said. "It will give you something to occupy your mind." Kate backed up, turning the car around. As they headed out of the driveway, she knew she was going to cry, and suspected that her tears were not entirely for Banny.

"I feel stupid and helpless," she said. "We've got you back, but now what? I'm terribly tempted to forget the whole thing, and just cling to our ordinary, privileged existence as to a life raft."

"I know," Reed said. "But you don't mean that. What I can't figure out is where to go from here. It's the end of the first act, and we haven't a clue about the rest of the play. The curtain has fallen, but the audience, thinking it's all over, has left, and the theatre is empty."

"At least we didn't tell Dorothy anything. Or did we?"

"We told her we didn't want her help anymore. Who knows what she'll make of that? Let's hope she'll put our behavior down to sadness over Banny. The question is, now what?"

Kate, shaking her head, kept her eyes on the road.

Eight

BUT the next day, someone appeared with an idea for the second act.

Reed had called from the office to say he was bringing someone home for a drink, someone who had an idea about the kidnapping. (Kate noticed that he always referred to it as *the* kidnapping, not *my* kidnapping, recognizing that it was as much hers as his.) The someone was named Emma Wentworth, and more would be explained when they met.

Emma Wentworth was the sort of woman whom Kate took to on sight. She had often tried to detail for herself this instant liking and had failed dismally. Or, put more sensibly, she had often come to like, indeed to cherish, women who did *not* make this kind of first

impression. First impressions were notoriously decep-
tive. Nonetheless, she warmed to Emma, who was
large, not fat, but large, imposing in manner and body.

Emma was also at home in her body, an important
factor, and had taken care with her appearance as
though she knew how it would, and should, repre-
sent her. She wore a dress, fitted on top and at the
waist, but with a full skirt, a dress that said: I'm
wearing a dress, but I am not wearing a power suit. I
have a decent figure for a large woman, but no desire
to flaunt my legs nor to worry about where they are
when I sit. I am intelligent, competent, reliable, and
funny. . . . Can a first impression have conveyed all
that? Well, of course, Reed had brought her home,
which said something, and had introduced her as a
professor, visiting at Reed's law school this semester.

Emma accepted a Scotch, yet another confirmation of Kate's instinctive liking, and began talking.
"Reed has told me about his adventure—in fact he
has told everybody, who told everybody else, in the
hope of stirring up some answers. I said Reed's adventure, but the adventure was, in fact, yours, which
I consider a vital point. One of my students, having
heard the story—somewhat embellished, as I subse-
quently learned, in the retelling—passed it on to me.
I dropped in on Reed because I thought I might be
able to help you, not with any particulars, but with
what I have learned after study of these right-wing
groups, how they operate, and how they can be dif-
ferentiated one from the other. Reed cut me off at the

start of my disquisition and suggested that I tell my theories to you too."

"I gave Emma the whole story, including the sordid details," Reed said. "I thought we could use some advice about those we were trying to flush out, and she might as well know it all."

Kate nodded.

"I've been studying right-wing groups," Emma said, "their motivations and their differences. One of the points we liberals miss is that those on the right agree when it comes to all modern forms of art—whether literature, entertainment, or even music—they all agree that its influence is debilitating, probably evil. As Wendy Steiner has put it"—she opened her notebook— " 'for the opponents of the liberal academy, complexity and ambiguity are merely mystifications, and contemporary art in fact compounds social disorder. The world's ills should be overcome instead by the enforcement of hierarchies and systems inherited from the past, with art'—and of course literature—'fulfilling its social mission by bolstering and justifying these systems.'* I keep those sentences around to quote, because they sum up neatly the bottom line for those on the far right."

"William Bennett, Allan Bloom, and Jesse Helms, in short," Kate said.

"Well, yes, as far as their ideas go, if one can accuse

*Wendy Steiner, *The Scandal of Pleasure: Art in an Age of Fundamentalism*, University of Chicago Press, 1995.

Jesse Helms of having anything describable as an idea. But my point to Reed and to you is that however much these right-wing people agree, their actions on behalf of their beliefs are quite distinct. While they would all, for example, like to have laws passed forbidding the kinds of art and teaching of modern ideas and concepts that undermine what they consider the fundamental values, they fight the likes of you and me, and everyone from those seeking abortions to the National Endowment for the Arts (which they have largely succeeded in eviscerating) in different ways. Much as we would all like to think so, the fact is that relatively few of those on the far right, outside of the militias and, I am tempted to say, those in politics or running for office, condone violent acts or acts such as those committed against Reed."

"What about those committed against Kate?" Reed asked.

"That's what is interesting. As far as I can discern, feeling against liberal academics runs pretty high, but to kidnap a woman's husband doesn't ring true to me as a neoconservative move given all the facts of this case. And I assume I have been given all the facts of the case?"

Kate looked at Reed, who nodded. "All of them," he said.

"Are you saying," Kate asked, amazement in her voice, "that they will murder a doctor who performs abortions, or organize militias to protect their property from the government, but they wouldn't set Reed or me up in the way that they did? One is acceptable, the other isn't?"

"It's not quite like that. Let's leave the militia groups out of this. They are mostly in the West or Midwest and couldn't possibly be directly involved in this sort of academic maneuver. Remember also, Kate, that those who commit murders—and that includes assassinations—are mentally ill fanatics whom those who wish to have a particular murder committed enlist for their purpose. Ray, Oswald, Sirhan Sirhan—these were all unbalanced fanatics egged on to their murderous acts. They weren't charter members of right-wing groups."

"All right, I'll give you that for the moment," Kate said. "Where does that leave us?"

Emma smiled. "I see you want me to skip the explanations and the political analysis and cut to the chase, as they say."

"Well," Kate said, "I suppose that's true, though I do find all you have to say intensely interesting. I hope you'll give us a chance in the future to learn more about your work; I mean that. It's just that, at the moment, I'm rather egotistically tense about our own situation. I don't want to think of Reed's being kidnapped all over again."

Reed took Kate's hand and spoke to Emma: "I suspect we're overeager to get to the bottom of this mess and clear it up, if we can. I'm sure Kate didn't mean to sound ungrateful to you for helping us, and I assure you that if she says she's interested in what you have learned and that she wants to know more about it, that is the simple truth."

"Point taken," Emma said. "No offense in the world. On to the chase." She put her notebook back into her bag, and seemed to pause a moment to collect her thoughts.

"Here's how I see it," she said. "You have two groups of people involved in the kidnapping. The lesser in importance are the students, both the boys who carried out the kidnapping of Reed, and the girls who kept him in their apartment and played their sexual games."

"But what about the boy who wrote the antifeminist letter to the college newspaper, and whose mother is a right-wing leader?" Reed asked.

"That's probably how the student group got involved. I rather doubt the mother of this boy had much to do with it. I could be wrong—keep in mind that mine are only guesses, though educated guesses— but I'll wager the mother, however intolerant of your sort of person, did not know of this plan."

"Harriet has been getting acquainted with her," Kate said. "She'll probably be able to find out if you are right. I'm pretty sure Harriet wouldn't have mentioned the whole kidnapping bit to the mother because she, Harriet, was pretending to be right-wing herself, and wouldn't have had any way to know about it."

"I'll be interested to hear her report," Emma said.

"And the second group?" Reed asked.

"Right-wing," Emma said, "but in my opinion, not a group of right-wingers, but an ultraconservative academic who has it in for Kate—therefore in all likelihood a member of Kate's English department. It could be someone in another department or in the administration, but I consider that unlikely. Whoever was behind this had to be near enough to Kate on a more or less daily basis to monitor her."

"Are you sure?" Kate said. "I mean—"

"No, I'm not sure. I may be miles off the mark, and this whole thing may have been planned by a militia group that has set up quarters in Central Park, or in some New York apartment. But none of this smells like right-wing group activity, except for the students— and they only in their motives, not in their actions, which were, I think, directed by someone else, and that someone a professor. After all, the boys and girls involved are all students."

Reed and Kate looked as though they might need a week at the very least to digest this.

"And if you're right, how do we find out which professor it is?" Reed asked.

"Ah," said Emma, "there you are on your own. I'm willing to bet a goodly sum that whoever he or she is is in Kate's department. But I don't know the cast of characters well enough, indeed at all, to even hazard a guess—except for this. Whoever it is dislikes Kate intensely, and probably not for personal reasons, not, that is, because you've done him or her some direct personal damage, but because by your presence in the department and your teaching of literature, you profoundly threaten what this individual holds dear, just as you threaten Bill Buckley and William Bennett and their political think-alikes. I'd suggest you begin by getting a list of the tenured members of your department—it may be someone without tenure, but I doubt such a person would take the risk, and anyway, we have to narrow the field at first. It can always be enlarged if necessary."

"Ours is a large department," Kate muttered in the tones of one announcing that Texas was a large state. "There must be at least thirty tenured professors. How do we know it wasn't a lawyer colleague of Reed's?"

"We don't." Emma was clearly trying to be patient. "If everything I've suggested turns out to be wrong, we start over. As I say, we have to start somewhere. And absent some vital bit of information that might result from your widespread storytelling, all my experience tells me to start with the English department."

The three of them sat in silence. After a few minutes, when neither Kate nor Reed spoke, Emma rose to her feet: "I'll be off then. Think about what I've said. It won't hurt to make a list of the tenured professors in the English department, and add a few details: who's on leave, is a known left-winger, was having a baby or an operation in the past weeks or months—all that sort of thing. Then, if you know anything of their ideas from their books, you might consider those with care. Do you happen to have an ardent Freudian among your colleagues?"

Kate stared at her. "Yes, we do. But why on earth . . . ?"

"I'm just being silly now," Emma said. "Pay no attention."

"I used to be silly," Kate remarked. "It's amazing how these Christian bigots can knock the silliness out of you. Why a Freudian?"

"Well, he went after Reed, didn't he? The woman, even if she is the enemy, isn't worthy of combat because she hasn't got a you-know-what, which is the absolute signifier."

If she had meant to make them laugh, she succeeded. Still chuckling, they walked her to the door. "Keep in touch," Emma said.

"By now I'm ready to suspect everybody," Kate said to Reed as they went back to the living room and poured themselves another drink. "For starters, what do you really know about Emma Wentworth?"

"I didn't just meet her today, you know," Reed said. "I'm on the committee that voted to invite her for a visiting professorship, so while I haven't known her personally for long, I certainly know her record and her reputation. Both are mighty impressive. She's known as an authority on right-wing groups, the organizations and funding that support them, and the legal possibilities of preventing some of their effects. Not," Reed added, "that there are many of those."

"Now that you mention it," Kate said, "I've always wondered why no one stops all those church groups, who do not pay taxes because they are religious, from busing their people to take part in political actions. Why doesn't someone stop that? If you're tax exempt, you can't be political, no?"

"Yes. But even the more liberal churches would fight any such action. They don't want their tax exempt status even to come up for questioning."

"I might have known. But Reed, do you really think it's likely to be a member of the English department? I know some of them are a little autocratic, and some of them are conservative to a degree, but I didn't think any of them were committed to the religious right. After all, this isn't South Carolina."

"You may find that some of your colleagues wish it were."

Kate was still uncertain about how to discover the political views of her colleagues, something she had never thought to question, at least not lately. She remembered that most of them, at least those who had touched on the matter at all, loathed Nixon and thought Ronald Reagan was a joke, a man who thought he had fought in World War II because he had made movies about it. Lately, however, politics within the department had been so fraught that national politics didn't seem to come up. At least, whenever she had lunch with a colleague, it was always gossip—about their department or people at other universities. Kate was continually astonished at how much some of her male colleagues knew about the personal lives of English professors from distant departments, and she had to admit she found the gossip amusing. But politics? They never seemed to gossip about that.

But then, the very next day, as she was leaving the campus, a professor she had never known well accosted her and demanded conversation. Nathan Rosen mainly taught undergraduates, at which he was reputed to be highly successful, particularly in survey courses, a realm of teaching Kate found, after her apprentice years, to be superficial and maddeningly repetitive. Her guilty dislike of these courses caused her to have great respect for those who agreed to undertake them year after year and did them well.

"Shall we get a cup of coffee?" Kate asked.

"I don't much like the restaurants around here," Nathan said. "I'm kosher." Almost inadvertently Kate looked up at his head. He was not wearing a yarmulke. He intercepted her glance. "I only wear it when I eat, and at certain other times," he said. "Not here. But I wanted to talk to you about a student who does wear his all the time. Could we go to my office?"

Nodding, Kate followed him, wondering if she was about to be accused of anti-Semitism. These days, students complained about the slightest remark that

115

could possibly be interpreted as an affront. On the whole, Kate understood the sensitivity of students from backgrounds unfamiliar to her, and was patient in trying to understand the cause of such sensitivity. But she had known Jews all her life, and certainly had never before been accused of insulting them. She felt herself growing angry even as Nathan opened the door to his office, walked in, and pointed to a chair. Kate sat.

"The student I mentioned said that you were patience personified with students of color, but that you were rude to him."

"Am I to know his name, or do you want me to answer anonymous charges?"

"His name is Krasner—Saul Krasner."

"Ah, yes," Kate said. "I know him."

"And, am I to assume, don't like him?"

"Well, he does seem to think he's God's gift to the world. I may have been impatient with him. Does that have to be because he's Jewish? I admit to not liking arrogance in students, particularly when it is allied with ignorance. To say nothing of the fact that he seems to assume that women ought not—how shall I put it?—be in any position to have authority over him. Perhaps you agree with that sentiment." It was not exactly a question, and Professor Rosen left it unanswered.

"I wasn't talking about women," he said. "I was talking about blacks. According to Mr. Krasner, you listened endlessly to some black man expounding on something, but had no time for him."

"Mr. Krasner does tend to interrupt other students and me; courtesy is not his most evident characteristic. But I'm sorry if I hurt his feelings, and I would certainly like to talk it over with him."

"The real question, Kate, is why are you, and so many others, patient with blacks and impatient with Jews and other white people?"

"I may have to plead guilty to being patient with those who are dealing with unfamiliar literature in an unfamiliar place, and who have the advantage of being able to give the rest of us, the other students and me, another point of view from which to consider the works we are studying."

"You're an advocate of multiculturalism."

"Nathan, I don't want to have a name-slinging argument with you. As I said, I'll be glad to talk over any offense I may have given with Mr. Krasner."

"And what do you think of Orthodox Jews, just for starters?"

"I don't know why I should answer that question, but assuming it to have been sincerely asked, I don't, personally, admire any fundamentalist religion. Every war that has ever been fought—well, certainly any war being fought today—is over religion. As a woman, I don't like the way women are viewed by fundamentalist religions of any kind. Also—"

"Let me ask you something?" Interrupting her answer to his question, Nathan leaned forward and pointed a finger at her. "You're sitting in the subway, not at rush hour. A group of adolescent black males gets on the train, talking loudly and jeering. Next stop, a group of guys from a yeshiva gets on, with yarmulkes and payes. Which group do you fear?"

"Good question," Kate said, wondering how often he had asked it. "My answer is, do you mean fear immediately or eventually?"

"What is that supposed to mean?"

"It's supposed to mean that, right at that moment, the group of black males is likelier than the group of Orthodox Jewish males to frighten or even molest me. But in the long run, I fear the boys from the yeshiva more."

"You're kidding!" And indeed, Nathan looked astonished.

"The young black males will go their separate ways. Perhaps, if as the richest country in the world we offer them and their families some support, they may even achieve something interesting. I can't guess what."

"I can," Nathan inserted.

"But," Kate continued, ignoring this, "I know exactly what the yeshiva males will be thinking for the rest of their lives, and maybe for the rest of their children's lives, and it's not a philosophy that I as a woman and a liberal find at all comforting. In fact, I fear it. Does that answer your question?"

"You're a bleeding do-gooder."

"Probably," Kate said, rising. "I've never understood why being called a do-gooder should be an insult. Your faith says somewhere that you may hate your neighbor, but if his cart is stuck in the road, you must help him to get it out. That's an approximate, not an exact, quote."

"Where did you pick that up?"

"Probably from all the humanist, do-gooder, liberal Jews I know. So long, Nathan." And Kate departed quickly, leaving Nathan Rosen still sitting there with his mouth open, his reply ready.

Kate was mixing martinis when Reed came home. He raised an interrogative eyebrow at her, and went to get the martini glasses.

"Don't tell me you've met a right-winger already, with murder and kidnapping in his or her eye?"

"Not exactly. I've been accused of anti-Semitism because I didn't respond with sufficient sympathy to an arrogant student who hadn't even read the assignment."

"He complained to you?"

"No. A Jewish colleague, by which I mean Orthodox Jewish. He seemed to think I was as bad as Hitler, except that I was nice to blacks."

"I don't blame Jews all that much," Reed said, tasting the drink. "Many blacks are openly anti-Semitic today, as is the radical right. It can't be easy."

"No, it can't," Kate said. "But do I really have to pretend to admire fundamentalist Jews any more than fundamentalist Muslims or the Christian right?"

"Well, how many Muslims and members of the Christian right do you have in your classes?"

"Enough of them to have managed to kidnap you. Oh, never mind, Reed. I get your point."

"The question is, would you prefer it as it was fifty years ago, with only WASP males, gentlemen all, of course, teaching in college, always supposing you were a WASP male too?"

"No, damn it, I wouldn't. Well, at least I may have eliminated one colleague from my roster. Thank heaven for that, anyway."

Nine

As Kate found the horrors of the previous days receding, she was pleased to discover herself capable of a return to her former personality, a return marked by a meeting with Leslie in the loft into which she had burst with the news of Reed's kidnapping. Only extreme panic had then allowed Kate so nonurban an indiscretion as "dropping in." Today's meeting had, as in ordinary times, been arranged in advance to take place after Leslie had completed her work for the day.

When Kate arrived, Leslie was still sitting in her studio, gazing at her unfinished work. It was an enormous canvas, and Kate admired it silently for some time. A mark of their friendship was that Kate

121

was allowed to see work in progress although not to comment unless asked.

"I think I've followed this whole sorry business from the beginning," Leslie said. "But just to clear my mind, tell me where you are at this very moment."

"Nowhere," Kate said. "That is, I've about decided that I agree with Emma Wentworth—that the right wing is not responsible for what happened, at least not alone responsible. I've been sifting through the list of the professors in my department, trying to decide which one would be likely to hatch this juvenile plot."

"Which *male* professor, I presume."

"Yes. I honestly can't see one of the women doing it. None of them particularly hates me, and since they're all, to a woman, married with children— that is, busy—I don't think they'd have either the time or the inclination for so extended and nasty a prank."

"That's probably right," Leslie said. "But I don't think you should eliminate women altogether. My guess is that the guilty one is not a professor. In fact, the whole point may be that she is not. I know you are convinced it's one of your male colleagues, driven to distraction by these changing times, but I've got other ideas. Want to hear them?"

Kate nodded. "That's why I'm here, among other reasons," she said.

Leslie had wandered about, gazing at her canvas

from various angles as she talked, but now she abandoned this and sat down on a stool opposite Kate. "I think you've got it all wrong," Leslie said.

"How?"

"The whole thing smacks to me of an envious woman, one who's known you a long time, or at least known about you for a long time, and is furious at your success, relative to her self-perceived failure, or lack of success."

"What makes you think so?" Kate asked.

"Personal experience, my dear—suffering and tumult, and the residue of a lonely life."

Kate stared at her friend. Leslie's was not a life Kate would have suspected of proffering loneliness. She had married young and stayed married for years; she had borne children, had painted when she could—which, lately, was most of the time—and had found in Jane a partner who offered her both a separate life and companionship. How little we know one another, Kate thought, and this is my best friend.

"Oh, not to look at," Leslie said, referring to her lonely life. "To look at it was crowded. Do you know, I've never lived alone. I even went right from marriage to life with Jane. But the loneliness stopped the moment I got out of the marriage."

"And how has that experience given you insight into Reed's kidnapping?" Kate asked. "It doesn't seem connected, not on the face of it, at least."

"Well, it's not as odd a connection as you think. I'm

123

one of those who's spent her life looking for a friend and for some success at my chosen calling. Let's say I look at you, and lo and behold, you've got a good relationship and you're good at your calling, and I don't have Jane or anyone else, and instead of painting, I've had to get a job illustrating greeting cards to support myself. You see what I mean?"

"Well," Kate said, "not exactly. I do think I'm getting there, but I'm not there yet."

"Okay. Let's forget art, which is not your field. Let's take up writing and teaching—that is, being a professor at a prestigious university and publishing well-received books."

"I'm not sure about the various adjectives," Kate said, "but I'm following. Go on."

"Look, nine-tenths of criticism, or reviewing, or whatever you want to call it, is, as you well know, composed largely of envy, rancor, and defense of one's own established ideas. But whether you're attacked or praised, you're taken seriously. Are you with me?"

"With you."

"Good. Now let's surmise a woman something like me, no real friends—which may be her fault or not—anyway, real loneliness, and no particular success in her profession, which I know you have assumed is academic, but just suppose it isn't. Suppose she didn't make it in academia, or only taught writing courses as an adjunct—whatever, I'm making this up. But the point is that she's now earning whatever living she can doing something she doesn't really respect and doesn't really respect herself for doing."

"Like what, for example?"

"How the hell do I know? That's what I'm suggesting you find out. Look into your past. Maybe she knew you. In fact, if you're the object of her revenge plan, her hatred, you must have known her at one time or another. The point is, Kate, I'm suggesting you forget the right wing and your colleagues in all this, and look for someone who may well be right-wing, may well be associated with the right wing, but whose animus is personal and personally directed."

"How do we know it isn't directed against Reed? He was the one kidnapped. He was the one grabbed off the streets and incarcerated and threatened with sexual exposure."

"True. But you were the one who was supposed publicly to condemn feminism, and you would have been the one held up to mockery if you had had to do that, and if they had got the pictures they were after, the ones of Reed with a nymphette. No, dear, shaming you was the object. The rest was fun and games, at least for those carrying it all out."

"And why get the right wing involved? I mean the whole tone was right-wing; they must have been a part of it."

"Obviously the right wing was glad to be used. It was carrying out their agenda. The question is, did they think it up? I know you have plenty of evidence of right-wing activities in the academic world, so

125

that you're quite willing to believe they could have thought this up. I don't blame you for coming to the conclusion you did. I'm just offering a different conclusion. I'm suggesting a personal animus directed against you as the originating source of all that happened."

Kate pondered this for a while. "What I don't get," she said finally, "is how you arrive at this idea of the culprit as friendless and frustrated professionally?"

"I told you: personal experience. Kate, throughout my old life, from the time my parents lost interest in me because they'd by then had the boy who really mattered, I was looking for a friend. I guess I was too earnest, or, what is probably nearer the truth, I had too funny an idea of friendship, probably modeled on stories of boys' companionships and adventures, and not realistic about them either. I remember at camp asking a girl to be my friend, and she said, 'We're all friends.' But we weren't. I wanted a special friend. Then, when I got married young, I thought: well, my husband is my friend. I kidded myself about that for quite a while. But husbands aren't friends; they're husbands, however friendly and supportive. It took the women's movement to make that clear, I guess. Meanwhile, I saw classmates from school and college who were getting somewhere, or I thought they were. I never seemed really to get time to paint. I tried studying art history, but even that didn't seem to satisfy; I wasn't really a scholar. If I hadn't left the marriage, and begun serious painting, and found Jane, and if I'd looked at you—successful, lots of friends and colleagues, with tenure, a good marriage, and, well, what looks like a pretty fulfilled life—I might be damn sore. You see what I mean?"

"More or less. You are, of course, wildly exaggerating the total satisfactions of my life. From time to time it seems quite purposeless to me, and full of petty professional squabbles, duties, and arbitrary decisions on the part of tyrannical administrators and pompous, aging, male professors."

"Of course it does. I'm asking you to look at yourself from the outside. I'm not saying that's how I see you; I'm saying how I might have seen you if things had been different with me."

"And the next step? I have to look in my past for a professional failure without friends? You don't ask much."

"Kate. Try being the detective you're always making yourself out to be. Obviously it's someone connected with what's happened, though I haven't an idea how she or he is connected. Whether it's someone behind the scenes or one of the players, I don't know. What I'm suggesting, dear friend, is that you start from the beginning, get over the mental stagnation caused by Reed's being kidnapped, and use your head. Is that clear enough? I could draw it for you, I suppose—well, a diagram anyway. How about a drink?"

"Lovely," Kate said, obviously deep in thought.

When Leslie returned with the drinks, she offered a toast to Kate and the new solution.

"Wasn't I a friend?" Kate asked. "We've known each other for, what, fifteen years? You never thought of me as a friend?"

"Oh, Kate. You came along after the friendlessness and the artistic frustration were, if not over, at least being defeated. Maybe meeting you even helped me. Did you ever think of that?"

"It can't be fifteen years."

"Now she's quibbling about years. Fifteen, fourteen, what's the difference? And the best part is when you've made one friend, you make more."

Kate twirled the glass around in her hand. "Do you really think," she asked, "that someone could go that far in trying to shame me?"

"Yes, I do. Not most people. If this whole mess hadn't happened, I'd never have thought of it; it's not the most likely thing in the world. But since it has happened, I'm just suggesting a possible explanation, at least as probable as the right wing or a demented professor whirling around on his or her own."

"I'll take it under serious consideration," Kate said. "Here's to professional jealousy as a solution."

"Give it a try," was all Leslie said, before they began to speak of other things.

Once home, Kate turned her mind to her past, trying to remember friendships from kindergarten on. It was amazing and a little troubling to discover how many people she had forgotten. School, camp, summer communities, travels, college—the task was daunting. Even if she could recall someone in particular whom she had once befriended, who had slipped away and not been encountered for years—and she couldn't—where would that get her? To trace every girlhood or student companion would be the job of months, perhaps years. Kate was not at all certain that Leslie was right in her surmise, but it certainly was worth thinking about. None of the other suppositions had yielded any helpful leads.

After a time she sought out Reed and told him Leslie's interpretation of the plot. Rather to her surprise, and a bit to her disappointment, he did not dismiss it out of hand.

"I've been beginning to question our ideas myself," he said. "The more I think about it, the less likely it seems to me that a professor would be involved, even some of the troglodyte types you've got in your department. Students, yes. This is exactly the kind of caper they could find themselves in. It resembles all the beastly games that fraternities seem to find so rewarding, in spirit if not in detail. The question is, as we have already seen, who got the students started, who arranged it all? Let's say the boys, given the ideas about pictures of sexual activities, recruited the girls. Who suggested that scheme to the boys? It's not that they couldn't have thought of it; of course they could

129

have, but for some reason I'm fairly sure they didn't. Why am I sure? Because it wasn't me they were after; it was you. College boys might have dreamed up the scheme as a way to get back at some male they loathed, but the point of this scheme was to shame you. Ruining my life was a case of collateral damage whoever was behind this probably never even considered."

"Fine," Kate said. "I'm with you. But where are you? We seem better at eliminating people than at identifying the culprits."

"If we assume it's a woman, and if we accept Leslie's explanation for her rage at you, then we might begin by assuming she's more or less your age."

"No kidding," Kate said, with more emotion than tact.

Reed ignored this. "Let's begin by limiting ourselves to women you met in school, college, or graduate school."

"Lovely. It should take me merely a year to compile such a list, let alone learn anything about where the women are now."

"Just list the ones you remember, the ones you had some sort of close contact with."

"Maybe I'll write the story of my life while I'm at it."

"You'll be right in style," Reed said. "Memoirs are what everybody's writing these days."

Kate in her turn ignored this. "You do realize," she said, "that we may never have met this woman—that she may not have shown herself in the course of this investigation. That she could be not only firmly behind the scenes, but determined to stay there."

"Quite possible," Reed admitted. "But she had to be in touch with someone we did meet, someone who has shown herself or himself."

"So we question all the girls, all the boys, all the people investigated by Harriet and Toni—Reed, we can't start that all over again."

"We can ask Toni and Harriet to start all over again. After all, that's their profession, isn't it? They're certainly as eager to figure this out as we are."

"True. I'll get on to them then." And she left Reed to his work.

The next day, therefore, she met with Toni and Harriet. She outlined Leslie's idea, said that she and Reed had found it plausible, or at least as plausible as anything else that had been suggested, so what they had to discover was who had been the originator of the scheme. Everybody had to be questioned as to who had talked them into taking part, from the kid who ordered the car onward. Kate was prepared to pay for Toni and Harriet's time for as long as it took.

"In short," Toni said, "we start all over again from the beginning."

"That's about it. Except," Kate pointed out, "I might at any moment get a clue, or become overpowered by the right memory, or have a brainstorm. And I don't intend to just sit by and cheer you two on. I think I'll start by going to see Dorothy Hedge again."

"Why do that?" Toni asked. "Do you think she might be the long-lost angry friend?"

"No, alas, I don't," Kate said. "But she is the sister of that goof who wrote the right-wing letter. Remember him? And besides, if you must know, I intend to tell her I'm coming, and ask her to borrow Banny from the woman who owns her. It can't hurt to have a little visit with Banny, can it?"

"It's not really advisable," Harriet said. "Like dropping in to see a child you've given up for adoption. A clean break is best, don't they think?"

"I'm not sure they do these days," Kate said. "I think adoptive mothers often know the biological mother and keep in touch with her. Anyway, I'm not adopting Banny. I'm just dropping in for a visit."

"Are you sure it's fair to Banny?" Toni asked.

"No, I'm not sure. I just want to see her again. It will probably turn out that she doesn't remember me at all, which will be crushing to me but not to her."

"Don't you think Reed or I should go with you?" Harriet said.

"Of course not. Reed may want to, in fact, but you two had better get going on the investigation. I've got classes and meetings all day tomorrow, but I think I can manage the next day. I'll ask Reed, if that makes you feel any better."

And having arranged certain financial details, and left a check to cover anticipated costs and payments, Kate left their office.

Ten

Two afternoons later Kate and Reed prepared to set out on their visit to Dorothy Hedge and Banny. Reed, like Harriet, had not altogether approved of the proposed visit to the puppy that was not theirs and which they ought, sensibly, to forget or to accept as an eccentric and unrecoverable event of the past. In the end, however, he had decided to accompany Kate—whether to provide her with emotional support at this canine crisis or to get another glimpse of Banny was not clear to Kate or to himself.

Kate had not again that day referred to Leslie's theories about an old friend of Kate's turned enemy, but she had worried Reed slightly by quoting Auden's lines, "Each life an amateur sleuth / Asking *who did it?"* Whenever Kate quoted Auden, Reed grew concerned.

They had called Dorothy Hedge the night before, and she had agreed to ask Marjorie about borrowing the dog. She too had issued a word of warning; indeed, she had tried to discourage the visit but had acquiesced upon their insisting that she at least leave the decision up to Marjorie. Late that night, Dorothy had called back saying that Banny and she were prepared to welcome them the next day.

Kate and Reed were almost out of the apartment when the telephone rang. After a moment's hesitation, Kate ran back to answer it. Harriet's voice was closer to frenzy than Kate had ever heard it.

"It's Toni." Harriet seemed almost to be gasping. "Someone tried to kill her."

"Where are you?" Kate asked.

"At the hospital. I found her in the office, lying on the floor. I thought she was dead, except that she was still bleeding. Dead men don't bleed—didn't someone once say that? I don't even know if it's true."

"Harriet," Kate said. "Tell me exactly where you are. We'll come."

"Roosevelt Hospital; the emergency room. It's—I think it's on Ninth Avenue."

"I know where it is. We'll be there, Reed and I. It won't be long."

Kate hung up. "Someone tried to kill Toni. Harriet's at the hospital. I said we would come."

"Is she going to be all right?"

135

"Oh lord, I didn't ask. Harriet said she was still bleeding when she found her. In their office."

The hospital was not far away. A taxi delivered them to the emergency entrance with commendable, if dangerous speed; Reed had said something to the driver. Kate dashed from the taxi, leaving him to pay, which seemed to be only a matter of thrusting some bills at the driver. Just like the movies, Kate thought, wondering if she was losing her mind to think that at such a moment. They found Harriet hovering amid a crowd of waiting people.

"Thank God you've come. They've taken her off to test her brain. I called the police, and that may have got her faster attention here; maybe the ambulance came faster. I don't know. Someone hit her all over the back of her head. She may die. The doctors weren't all that hopeful."

Reed spotted an empty chair. "Sit down," he said. "Tell her to sit down"—this to Kate. They urged Harriet into the chair.

"She ought to have tea with lots of sugar," Kate said. "That's what the English take."

"I don't need anything; I've had something," Harriet said.

"Tell us about it then." Reed squatted down until his face was on a level with hers. Kate leaned over Harriet's chair and took her hand. For the first time since she had met Harriet, Kate was aware of her friend's age. Kate had always known her to be in her sixties—or even, by now, beyond—but never before had Harriet looked aged, tired, and fragile.

"Tell us what happened," Kate said, holding Harriet's hand. "Start at the beginning. Take it slowly."

Harriet sighed, more of a gasp, really, as though she had been holding her breath and her body needed oxygen. She seemed to be searching for a handkerchief, and Reed gave her his. She wiped her eyes, and held the handkerchief to her mouth as she talked.

"I had gone to the bank," Harriet said. "We had spent the morning talking about how we would start again, trying to find some new clue that might lead us to whoever was behind this. Actually," she added, as though she had just thought of it, "Toni seemed rather distracted. We needed cash, and she urged me to go to the bank—you know, the teller machine. It's not far, but of course there's always a line around lunchtime. I could hear Toni starting to make some phone calls as I left, setting up some meetings and so forth. I didn't really listen. There was a long line at the bank machine, and when I came back, when I opened the office door, there she was. I thought she was still bleeding, which made me hope. I called the police and an ambulance, the ambulance first but they came at the same time. Then I called you, I mean right after calling the police and ambulance. The police looked at me very suspiciously. I think they're keeping an eye on me. They asked a lot of questions. The police don't especially like private eyes. In books the private eye is always a tough guy, maybe an ex-policeman, and they, the police, get on with him. I think the only thing that kept them from taking me in was my age, and that Toni was my partner."

It seemed that having started talking, Harriet could hardly stop. Indeed, all that lessened the flow was the approach of a doctor.

He looked at Kate and Reed with what might have been hope. "Are you related to the patient?" he asked.

Reed stood up. "No," he said. "We just knew her professionally. She worked with our friend here." He indicated Harriet.

"So she's not related either," the doctor said, glancing at his chart. "We need to contact her relatives."

All three of them looked at Harriet.

"I haven't any idea where they are," Harriet said. "Oh, dear. When she came to work at the law school she said her family was from Idaho, but that her parents were dead. She's never mentioned anyone else. I don't even know where in Idaho. I've never even heard of most places in Idaho." She began to cry, pushing Reed's handkerchief against her eyes.

Reed moved so that he was facing the doctor, an obviously competent, probably professional man facing another professional man. The doctor decided that Reed was the one to talk to.

"This woman is an old friend of ours," Reed said, "She was, as I've said, the partner of the assaulted woman. For the moment at least, we're the only people who can be consulted about her. Could you let us know her condition?"

"Critical," the doctor said, with (Kate hoped, overhearing them) more blunt frankness than he might have offered the family. "She was beaten on the back of the skull with a heavy instrument. Our guess is that the person who attacked her left her for dead. We're dealing with brain trauma here, but we're rather better at that than some hospitals; we get more practice. There wasn't time to wait for all the forms to be filled out. Since the police were involved, perhaps they'll locate some relatives; I gather she wasn't married."

Reed shook his head.

"So we'll just wait and see. But I warn you, she may remember nothing of what happened. With brain damage, that's often the case."

"May we leave you our names," Reed asked, "just in case you want to reach someone? I take it you already have the information about her partner here."

The doctor looked as though he was about to refuse, but Reed, holding the man's gaze, handed over his card.

"Ah," said the doctor, glancing at it. "A law professor." And with that he rushed off.

"Why don't you go home with us now?" Kate said. "We can let them know where you'll be."

"I want to stay here," Harriet said. "Maybe they'll let me see her. Maybe she'll know I'm here, even if she's unconscious. They say people in comas know you're there."

Kate decided not to insist that Toni might not be in a coma. She didn't, in fact, know whether one fell into a coma immediately after such a blow, or only after a time. Around them in the emergency waiting room, there was constant movement and the almost palpable aura of anxiety and fear. Kate looked at Reed to see if he had a suggestion.

"Look," he said. "There are two seats over there. Why don't you two sit in them and wait? There might be news soon. I'll go and see if I can get some information—perhaps find out where we are with this, and persuade them to let Harriet leave." He glanced toward a policewoman standing at the edge of the room. She was watching them as they moved toward the now empty seats. Harriet, after all, Kate realized, was a suspect. Was the person who found the body often a suspect? She nodded to Reed. What they did not say to one another, because it was understood, was that Reed still had connections from the years he'd worked in the district attorney's office. Maybe by now he had them somewhere else too.

"We'll wait here," Kate said, "unless they tell us enough so that we can leave. In that case, we'll be at home." She urged Harriet into one of the seats and took the other.

Reed touched her shoulder and left. Kate saw him stop to speak a moment to the policewoman, then depart.

For what seemed like hours, Harriet told Kate every detail of finding Toni on the floor of the office, accounted for every minute she had been absent from the office and allowing, by her absence, the attack to happen, and turned over for her own sake, if not for Kate's, every possible explanation of what had occurred, other cases they were working on, and Kate's case. Kate had no idea how much time had passed when the doctor reappeared. Kate had let Harriet talk, partly because she thought it would help her, provided she didn't get into the habit of repeating it endlessly—thus indicating all kinds of possibly neurotic responses—and partly because she, Kate, was really eager to hear all the events and conditions that afternoon.

And then the doctor reappeared. Harriet stopped in the middle of a word. They gave him their ferocious attention, half hope, half dread.

"I think your partner's going to be all right," he said to Harriet. "At least a lot better than we had any right to hope. She's already regained consciousness, which is the best possible sign, although she's not yet responsive. She may not remember anything that happened, even if she's able to talk and recognize people and remember other things. That's usual. In time, if all goes well, her memory of what happened when she was attacked may come back. There was a clot, but we found it and got it out. We have a doctor here who's studied brain trauma, which most neurologists don't." Here he seemed to decide he was

141

talking too much, whether from fatigue or relief or pride, and turned away.

Harriet reached out and touched his arm as he was retreating. "Are you saying she'll be all right? That she won't be—well, crippled or deaf or anything?" Or a vegetable, Kate wanted to add, but didn't because of Harriet.

"I can't make promises. The signs are good—that's all I can tell you. Excuse me, now."

Harriet seemed about to reach for him again, but Kate seized her outstretched arm. "For a doctor he was amazingly communicative," Kate said. "Most of them either utter telegraphic nonsense or ask what should be done with the body. Just be grateful. I think he was telling us we could and should leave now. Let's go home. You ask that nice policeperson if you can go, give her my address if she asks, and I'll go and make sure they have our number should there be any reason to call, though I think Reed gave it to them. I'll just make sure. Go on, now," Kate said, shoving Harriet ever so slightly. She had never seen Harriet anything but in absolute control of herself, and she felt, though it annoyed her to realize it, like a child who has discovered an idol is not omnipotent. Kate walked toward the woman at the reception desk and waited for a chance to leave her number once again. More than anything, she needed a few minutes to collect herself.

By the time they reached home, Harriet—who'd been shaking in the taxi beyond anything caused by the driver or potholes—was near to tears, which astonished Kate. Harriet had been through some bizarre adventures in her life but had not collapsed; she had mustered her determination and will and accomplished what needed to be done. In this case, clearly, she was out of control; nothing she might do, at least nothing that occurred to her at this time, could alter these events. Regret joined with powerlessness induces despair.

Kate offered single malt Scotch, Harriet's favorite, but was not surprised to observe that the drink had little effect on Harriet's mood or spirits. There are, Kate had long ago learned, certain worries that neither Scotch nor prescription drugs can touch, at least not right away. But Kate plied the whiskey in the hope that, exhausted, Harriet might give way to sleep.

By the time Reed returned, Harriet had at last laid her head on the arm of the couch and dozed off. Reed suggested that they leave her to rest undisturbed, but Kate thought her likelier to remain asleep if she had, even subconsciously, the sense that she was still in the midst of things. Harriet, at that moment, opened her eyes, saw Kate, and closed them. They heard her breathing become even again.

"How do you know these things?" Reed asked.

Kate shrugged. "I know some things; you know others. Between us, we cover a certain amount of ground. I only hope we can make the combination work with this awful mess. What did you learn, if anything? The doctor, by the way, is sounding as close to hopeful as doctors ever sound when they're being honest, but I gather she has a long way to go before she's out of danger."

"You haven't changed your opinion of the medical profession, I see," Reed commented, when she had told him of the doctor's report. "They sound as though they've done a pretty good job in this case."

"I'm willing to wait and see. I'll admit that much. What's your news?"

Reed had just opened his mouth to speak when the telephone rang. They had brought their cordless phone into the living room and Reed answered it immediately. Kate glanced over at Harriet, but she hadn't budged.

Reed, meanwhile, was oozing apologies. "A crisis," he was saying. "I can't go into it now. We must keep the line clear. No, not in the family. We'll call as soon as we can, and please forgive us." He disconnected by pressing a button and pushed in the aerial. Inappropriately, Kate thought of how satisfying the gesture of firmly replacing the receiver used to be. "Dorothy Hedge," Reed said. "Wondering what had become of us. You heard my end."

"What about Banny? Will Dorothy Hedge keep her awhile? I don't know why on earth I should think of that, under these circumstances."

"I didn't ask. I think she was going to say something else, but I wanted to get off before I had to answer any more questions. Remember, we don't know who tried to kill Toni."

"But why on earth . . . ?" Kate began.

"Everyone who knew Toni or knew of her is a suspect at this moment. Do you want to hear my news?"

"I hate it when you become officious, but yes, I do. My main question is: did the attacker leave her for dead or not? Did he or she think Toni was dead?"

"The first question I asked," Reed said, his tone praising her and making up for sounding officious. "They can't be sure, but the detective, whose instincts I've learned to trust, thinks they did leave her for dead. This suggests it was someone not used to battering people, someone who panicked, who was running scared. I think that's a good guess."

"That ought to assure them that it wasn't Harriet, oughtn't it?" Kate asked, glancing at the couch. They had managed to lift Harriet's legs onto the couch and they had covered her; she was deeply asleep. Perhaps, Kate thought, Scotch had worked in its own way after all. "I mean, she'd hardly have called the police if she wasn't sure Toni was dead. They can't really suspect Harriet, can they?"

"Not for long, I hope. What we've got to find is what motive anyone would have had for attempting to kill Toni. It's perfectly possible it's from another part of her life and has nothing to do with us, but somehow I doubt that. When Harriet wakes up, we'll ask what else she and Toni were working on. Someone will have to go over the papers in their office. Either

Harriet will let me do that with her, or the police will get a warrant. But assuming that Toni was attacked because of your case, I think we ought to get all of that straight in our minds."

"Whatever do you mean?"

"We changed our tactics. We decided to follow Leslie's suggestion. In short, we altered the whole direction of the investigation. Not twenty-four hours after you discussed this new direction with Toni and Harriet, Toni was attacked. I'm inclined to see a connection. At the very least, I want to assure myself and you that there isn't one."

"You're suggesting," Kate said, after turning this over in her mind, "that whoever was responsible for kidnapping you, for trying to force me to repudiate feminism, and all the rest of it, got so frightened by the idea of our hitching onto Leslie's idea that they tried to murder Toni? What would be the point?"

"Simple fear—an hysterical response. An attempt to provide a red herring, distract us from one trail to another. It's all guesswork for now. Maybe someone feared that something or other that Toni had happened upon might lead her to the person behind all this. Who knows? One possibility is that she or he meant to incriminate Harriet, thus putting the whole firm out of business, but something interrupted her, which is why Toni isn't dead."

"Ye gods," Kate said. She realized that she had to face what she had been carefully avoiding while concerning herself entirely with Harriet. "In other words, I'm responsible for what happened to Toni."

"In a way, you are," Reed said. He never tried to hide the truth from her, which was, she supposed, what above everything she loved him for. "But that's like saying if the police are shot by a person burglarizing a store, the store owner is to blame. Toni worked as a detective, a licensed detective. Risks are part of the job. And she must have let whoever it was into the office. I haven't asked Harriet about that yet, but New Yorkers don't leave their office doors open unless there's a receptionist just inside, and even then there's usually a buzzer to release the door."

"I hadn't thought of that." Kate looked abashed. It was startling to realize the extent to which she hadn't really begun to think at all.

"So," Reed said, "what you've got to do is work even harder on trying to locate this woman whose possible motive Leslie described. She may not be the key to the whole thing; she may only be a small part of it. But the coincidence, the timing of the attack on Toni, certainly suggests the possibility of a connection. My instincts tell me the solution lies in that direction."

"Reed, we don't even know if she exists. And if she does exist, how on earth am I going to think of her? The whole thing's absurd. We need a few clues, at least. My God, she may even go back to nursery school, and I can't remember anyone I've met later than the last decade—and not most of those."

"Nonsense. What did you do when you thought it might be a professor in your department? You made lists: probable, improbable, impossible."

"There are only thirty professors in the department. Maybe thirty-one—I haven't counted lately."

Reed ignored this. "If you made such an impression on her that she has seethed with it ever since, you must at least have some memory of her, however recessed. You'll have to dig it out. It hardly seems likely that a casual remark or a one-time meeting is the cause of all this. It's possible, but if that's the case we're dealing with a lunatic"—at Kate's raised eyebrows, he amended this—"with an insane rather than an obsessed person. You know what I mean. In that case, we may never find her or him, or this may have nothing to do with you. But if the same person is behind this and the former caper, and that's what I believe, the sooner you can come up with a list of possibilities, the better."

"Going back to nursery school?" Kate almost sneered.

"Let's start a bit later—say, high school. On through college, jobs, boyfriends, travels—I'm suggesting the situations in which you and she may have both been involved."

"Well, thanks for leaving out childhood anyway. I'm bored to death with childhoods. That's all anyone seems to write about these days. There's a fancy new theorist people are reading in lit crit circles named Adam Phillips. I recently looked at a book of his called *On Flirtation*, and he quotes something from Philip Larkin that I endorse most heartily."

Reed, who earlier that day had been distressed by her quoting of Auden, took hope now from her return to her customary patterns of thought. "I know you admire Philip Larkin's poetry, but I thought you were still reading a biography of him."

"That was last year."

"I can never keep up with your reading."

"Some of us read a lot, fast. Some of us read slowly, a few pages in bed at night before drowsiness overcomes us."

Reed smiled to see her old habits of speech reappearing. She smiled back at him.

"The quote from Larkin is relevant," she said, understanding his relief. "He said this to an interviewer: 'Whenever I read an autobiography I tend to start halfway through, when the chap's grown up, and it becomes interesting.' That's how I feel about my life. So I'll do a hasty survey of high school and college and then concentrate."

"You'd better concentrate from the beginning," Reed said. "We're looking for a murderer, even if it's one who failed, as we hope. Remember that. Sorry, I'm sounding officious."

There was no further news from the hospital about Toni that night. Harriet woke up and eventually agreed to be put to bed and to swallow a sleeping pill and a bit more Scotch. When all was quiet Kate went to call Leslie.

"A fine mess you've gotten me in," she said.

"Remembering your past, are you?"

"Yes, damn it," Kate said. And told her about Toni. They talked about that for a time, Kate asking again for reassurance that Leslie's analysis of the situation would turn out to be anywhere near the mark.

"It's just a guess, a supposition, a trial balloon," Leslie said. Kate could picture her in her studio, perched on a stool with her legs looped around its legs. She often retreated to the studio in the evening to brood over her painting and contemplate tomorrow's work. "The worst that can happen is that you'll waste some hours making lists and remembering. Who knows, it may all turn into a best-selling memoir, like Gore Vidal's."

Kate decided to let that pass. "The real problem is that I can't imagine anyone getting that angry, let alone staying that angry so long, or actually planning this whole mess."

"That's your personality," Leslie said. "Quick anger, short stew, complete forget. Well, you've got to stop forgetting just now. And don't underestimate anger in women. Hold on. I'm going to put down the phone and get a book."

"What book?"

"Just hold on." And Kate heard the receiver being put down and Leslie's footsteps. It seemed a good while till she returned. "Sorry," she said. "I had trouble finding the book. It's *Little Women*."

"*Little Women!*" Kate shouted.

"Here it is," Leslie said, ignoring this. "This is Marmee speaking. You remember Marmee—good as gold, patient as Griselda. She is speaking to Jo, of course. Who else would understand her? She says: 'I am angry nearly every day of my life, but I have learned not to show it; and I still hope to learn not to feel it, though it may take me another forty years or so.' Kate, women like you and me have learned to express anger, not to turn it inward, to turn it into depression, but to let it out. Some would say too much, but that's not the point here. If even Marmee could feel that angry, if Louisa May Alcott knew that much about anger, can you doubt what a woman's anger can do in someone a lot less angelic than Marmee?"

"How on earth did you remember that passage?" Kate asked.

"It comforted me once, long years ago, when I was reading *Little Women* to my children."

"I'll be damned," Kate said. "Okay, okay, you've made your point. You've definitely made your point."

Eleven

Toni continued to mend. The reports were encouraging: she had opened her eyes, responded to questions, assuring them that she knew her name. The doctors still felt certain she did not as yet remember anything of what had happened in the office the day she was attacked, and Reed's reports on the progress of the police were hardly helpful. Reed had once told Kate that the hardest murder to solve would be one in which someone hit a stranger over the head and disappeared. Motive and connection to the victim were what, in the end—together of course with all the marvelous new technology—trapped most murderers or those who attempted murder.

"How do we know whoever it was didn't just want to put her out of commission for a while?" Kate had asked. "Is there any reason to suppose that the assailant intended Toni to die?"

"Nothing I would want to demonstrate to a jury, at least at this point," Reed said. "My guess is that murder was intended, but the person, whoever he or she was, did not know exactly how much force was needed, and probably panicked in the end, rushing out before making sure of Toni's condition."

"Reasons?"

"As I say, hardly convincing evidence. But if someone walks into an office, hits the occupant over the back of the head, probably with a baseball bat or something like it, and then rushes out, the supposition has to be what I guessed."

"How do you know he or she rushed out?"

"The evidence is clear. Nothing else was touched except the doorknob. He or she wore gloves. The body wasn't touched in any way, even superficially, to determine its condition. And Harriet came in quite soon after the assault—the doctors tell us that. I think the assailant fled as fast as possible, disturbing nothing in the office, and not waiting around. In fact, Harriet probably saved Toni's life."

"They don't still suspect Harriet, do they?"

"They suspect everyone till they make an arrest, and sometimes even after that. I think you'd better face the fact, Kate, that there is quite a case to be made against Harriet."

"You can't be serious."

"I may not be, but the evidence is. Consider: she

says she went out to get cash, and we know she did indeed do just that, since ATMs kindly record the time and the amount of every transaction. Now it is, as you will readily see, easy enough for someone else, with the card and knowledge of the password or identifying number, to get money and leave the same record, thus providing a spurious alibi. No, no, don't interrupt. I'm not saying that's what Harriet did, but my assurances or yours would hardly satisfy the police. The police did, however, persuade the bank—no easy matter, that—to give them the names of those who had made deposits or withdrawals at the time Harriet did. Interviewed, some of these people described Harriet sufficiently well to assure the police that she was indeed there. A substitute made up to look like her might have been possible, but happily that occurred to no one but me, inspired by you and your peculiar adventures. That sort of thing happens in your world, doesn't it?"

Kate glared at him. "Go on. If you're trying to upset me, you're succeeding."

"Sorry. Harriet says she stopped in the women's room on the way back from the bank, not knowing that Toni was lying in the office, bleeding to death. She says there was another woman in there, and the police are canvassing the other offices on the floor to see if they can find the woman. But of course she could have been a client or a visitor. That's still up in the air. The point is that if Harriet didn't stop in the

154

rest room, she had ample time to attack Toni, leave the office, and return to find her."

"And what are supposed to be Harriet's motives in this odd drama?"

"Who knows. Partners falling out, discoveries as yet unknown to us. Whenever there's an attempted murder where burglary or sexual assault is not the purpose, the police are likely to suspect someone connected to the victim."

"It makes no sense," Kate observed, trying to keep her voice from rising. "Harriet could have killed Toni in a million other ways on a million other occasions. Besides, if Harriet wanted to commit a murder she would be far cleverer about it. She loves intrigue—you know that."

"She could just have been clever enough to figure out that that's what everyone would figure. As I've already mentioned, the murderer who hits and runs is the hardest to unearth. No"—he held up a hand as Kate looked alarmed—"I don't think Harriet's in serious trouble, unless, of course, she decides to try to solve this herself and gets in the way of the police or, worse, the would-be murderer. But my faith is based on what I know of her, and what you know of her. I think perhaps you had better let her know, in somewhat vague terms, that she's something of a suspect."

"I'll call her. If I know Harriet, she's already figured this out, and will mention it to me, unless she's in one of her protective moods. But I'll insist on a face-to-face encounter. That's harder to wiggle out of."

Kate did, in fact, call Harriet, but was able only to leave a message. The message was urgent, while revealing nothing of the trouble on Kate's mind. There was nothing more she could do, at the moment.

"Meanwhile," she told Reed as he was leaving, "I'll labor here at the task you and Leslie have given me. I know everyone in the world is writing a memoir at this very moment, but it does seem unfair that I, the only person with no interest in the past, have to dig it up this way."

Reed adopted the look of one who is determined to discuss a certain subject no more—a look, Kate sometimes thought, peculiar to husbands.

Leslie was, if not less insistent, more helpful. She turned up at Kate's as Reed was leaving, having offered her assistance in getting Kate started on her unwelcome task. She insisted on getting right to work, waved Kate to her desk, sat down in Kate's lounge chair, and started suggesting categories.

"College," she said.

"Impossible," Kate responded promptly.

"Never mind impossible. Did you have any close friends there, or even constant companions? Roommates? People you sat next to in class?"

"Leslie, for heaven's sakes, this was thirty years ago, and I haven't given it a thought since."

"You must have kept up with someone."

"I had three good friends in college. The closest was a pediatrician here in New York. She died of breast cancer a few years ago. Surely you remember. I miss her still, and would gladly suspect her of murdering someone if it would bring her back."

"Of course I remember. What about the other two?"

"One is a therapist in Minneapolis, and is far too busy to be popping in and out of New York. She's very good at what she does and is old-fashioned like me. That is to say, we write letters and talk on the phone. Lately, we've taken up e-mail. Any more details necessary?"

"Go on."

"The third is an Episcopal priest in Pennsylvania, and I talk to her a lot too. If she murdered anyone, it wouldn't be Toni; it would be someone in the Episcopal hierarchy. As to the other 'companions' from college, I can't see any of them carrying resentments. True, I don't go to reunions, but surely that isn't a sufficient motive for kidnapping and murder?"

"We're not looking for a 'sufficient' motive, you idiot. That's just the point. We're looking for something that's seethed and seethed and grown into an obsession that hasn't anything to do with reason. So stop looking for logic here. Did you go right on to graduate school after college?"

"No. I took a year off and worked on Wall Street. Not exactly *on* Wall Street. Metaphorically speaking."

"Were you out of your metaphoric mind?"

"Probably. When I became twenty-one, I had to face the fact that I had an income that would have

supported at least half of all the families in America.
I decided that I had to understand how it was earned."

"Rather like Lord Peter Wimsey watching a hanging, since that's where all the people he captured
ended up. Unless, of course, they shot themselves like
proper gentlemen in the library of their club. What
did you learn, if anything?"

"I worked in a brokerage house, temporary secretary. One of my brothers got me the job. He thought
it might make me into more of a Republican, I guess.
It didn't. But it did make a lot of things clear. Do we
really want to go into this now, or ever? I met no one
there who didn't either pity me or ignore me. They
pitied me because they knew my brothers. There
were very few women above the rank of secretary
then, and I don't think there's one of them who re-
tains the slightest memory of me that year."

"On to graduate school. Let's tread a little more
slowly. No dismissive remarks or waves of the hand.
I have a strong suspicion that this may be where you
met her. And of course she may not have been there
for long."

"You're still convinced it's a woman?"

"For now. I just don't see it as a male scheme, not
in those circles. It might be Rush Limbaugh's idea of
a great joke, as the boys and girls thought it a good
joke, but . . . why don't we just assume for now that
it's a woman. Let's start with a list of every woman
who was in graduate school with you."

"You must be mad."

"Trust me. Have you collected your transcripts according to directions from your bullying friend Leslie?" Kate waved them at her. "Okay, give them to me. Let's go class by class, lecture by lecture, seminar by seminar. I'll read out the class, you write down every woman who was in it whom you can remember— never mind whether you can come up with her name or not. She may have changed it five times since, anyway."

"Leslie—" Kate began, groaning.

"Leslie me no Leslies. Survey of English poetry."

"That was a lecture with hundreds of people in it and section men, as we called them then. They *were* all men, a condition about which I never thought I would say thank God."

"Whom did you sit next to?"

"Different people every time. Leslie, if someone is going berserk and trying to murder Toni because I one day happened to mention that I didn't care for Milton, we might as well give up this minute."

"All right, other classes. Start making lists."

Kate stared at the transcripts, startled to discover the courses she had taken, and how little she remembered of them. The seminars, limited in number, long and intensive meetings once a week, were more memorable. "There weren't that many women in them," she said as she reconstructed the class lists. "Isn't it odd, I can remember the rooms where we met, where we sat around the tables, often in the same place, who talked a lot, who talked little or not at all, and the papers each of us wrote and all of us read. I can actually connect the people with the papers, even if I can't come up with their full names. Memory is odd, indeed."

"Any women who hated your guts because you didn't approve of their views on *Jane Eyre*, or loathed you for any reason whatever? Or pretended to like you and then turned mean?"

"What you don't seem to recognize, Leslie, is that if they did hate me I didn't know it or don't remember it."

"You don't remember anyone of the female persuasion in graduate school who didn't like you?"

"Not especially. Somehow all these likes and dislikes didn't come into it, or if they did, I don't recall them. Graduate students get up much more steam over their professors than their fellow students. If you don't like a fellow student, you just shrug. At least, that's how I remember it, and that's my impression from graduate students today. Of course, gay students hate the homophobes, and I suppose vice versa, but I don't belong in either category and never did."

"You're not exactly being helpful, Kate, as I hope you realize. You've told me stories of women who misjudged you, or blamed you unfairly, or whatever. If I can remember them, surely you can. There was one woman who wanted you to push her anthology for a doctorate, and bad-mouthed you when you didn't, or couldn't, or wouldn't. Then there's the woman who didn't get a job, and the men told her it was because of you."

"Yes, that turned out to be a common trick, along with telling men you couldn't hire them because you had to hire a woman. Sometimes it was true, but very rarely. I know the cases you're talking about, but I can't see either of them—"

"Kate. Look at me. Try to get this through your thick head and stubborn resistance: somebody, probably some woman, hates you, and for personal, not political reasons, though she's willing enough to support political views loathsome to you. I thought I'd be able to help you, but I see I was wrong. All you're doing is using me to argue against. I'm leaving now. I'd like to stay and have a drink and talk about other things, God knows I would, but you've got to get your mind working on this problem. Call me when you've got one or more possibilities."

"Blackmail, pure and simple. I wouldn't have thought it of you, Leslie."

"Call it what you want. Once you have even the sniff of a trail, I'll come and help. Try to remember: you came as close to collapsing when they snatched Reed as I've ever seen you; they've tried to murder a detective you hired and damn near succeeded. So put your memory to work. I know it isn't easy to come to terms with the fact that someone hated you enough to do all this, but that's where we are. All right?"

"I still think it's blackmail," Kate said, but Leslie

161

had already left Kate's study and closed the door behind her.

Kate was still searching for excuses to do something else when the phone rang. It was Harriet. She said that she was on her way to see Toni, now allowed brief visits, and would come by to see Kate afterward. Kate was filled with a sudden impulse to warn Harriet about Toni (and Toni about Harriet), but contained herself. "I'll see you soon, then," she said.

Stretching herself out on the couch, Kate reflected that she was, in fact, less worried about Harriet than she might be. Not, Kate realized with some shock, because she was confident Harriet could not have killed Toni. Harriet, Kate believed, was able and likely to do whatever she considered necessary for whatever profound reason struck her with sufficient force. What Harriet was not capable of, Kate knew, was pretending to the fear on Toni's behalf she had exhibited at the hospital and in the telephone call summoning Kate and Reed. Harriet would be likelier, if she wanted to murder someone, to do so and then turn herself over to the authorities, or at least disappear. She would not stay around to pretend worry and concern with the skill of an accomplished actor.

There was, of course, always the worry that Kate, knowing this, might not be able to convince the police of it; she knew all too well, from Reed and others, how eager the police were to find a culprit and do what was necessary—not all of it always ethical—to get a conviction. But worry accomplished nothing.
162

Harriet would arrive in an hour more. Kate might as well, in the interim, be trying to imagine when and how she had inspired sufficient hatred to lead to Reed's kidnapping and the demands upon her which followed it.

She thought of Banny, who might, had she still been here, have jumped up on the couch and shared it with Kate. Kate picked up a pillow and held it to her chest, as though it were Banny. She gave up the struggle to remember, or even to imagine, some woman who hated her enough to have engineered the whole stupid plot, and let her thoughts wander where they might.

It was not often that Kate half dozed, half dreamed in this fashion, but her body and mind recognized a different kind of exhaustion, the result of Reed's kidnapping and all that anxiety. With her arms around the pillow, and her eyes closing, she wondered if age, which she had not thought of very much in recent years, was catching up with her. Had her resiliency been depleted? Had new terrors been evoked?

Well, if she thought of it, she had never before had someone she loved and had lived with threatened. Her life had held, it seemed to her, fewer turmoils than most. What had threatened her, if indeed she had ever felt truly threatened, had been not violent emotions, but from time to time a sense of the purposelessness of existence, of the lack of reason for so much that occurred. It was a sin of the spirit, she knew; a failure of faith in the rightness of the universe—of

God, in short. Yet she doubted that acedia was limited to agnostics or to those who had lost their faith. Indeed, she knew it was not. This sense of the pointlessness of life was far likelier suddenly to assault those whose lives were, on the whole, satisfactory, but who felt the lack of something beyond these much-to-be-envied satisfactions. It was what someone she used to know called divine discontent.

Who? It was Moon, all that long while ago. "Be mellow," he used to say, "or use the trouble to move on to something worthwhile or to better thoughts."

And, suddenly, she remembered an enemy she had made, the only enemy she could remember, thinking little enough of it at the time, glad to be rid of an acquaintance so mean-spirited, glad above all to be rid of such a person for a relative. Heavens, she thought, that it should have been my family after all!

Twelve

IT was the Sixties; of course it was.

The Fansler family had rented a summer house on the Maine coast from a cousin. The house was on the sea, and it came complete with tennis court and a swimming pool for those who scorned the waves. The nominal host and hostess were Kate's oldest brother, Lawrence, and Janice, his proper wife—indeed, Kate never thought of her in any other way. Janice always knew the right thing to do and did it. She maintained, furthermore, that all would go well if everybody simply did what was expected of them "in the position in life to which God had called them" (though it was Kate who had always added that last, Victorian phrase, which perfectly explained the woman's views even if she would not, in this day and age, have put it that way).

Kate's younger brother was a guest that weekend, together with his wife and young children and their nanny. Kate had agreed to attend this gathering at the insistence of her middle brother, whose engagement was being celebrated. Since he was the only brother Kate talked to in any terms other than perfunctory and coolly polite, she had agreed to his pleas to help see him through this ordeal: the family was destined to approve of his fiancée and he needed Kate's support. The family's approval, Kate understood, was even more daunting than their disapproval would have been.

Kate had, most unusually, for she avoided her family as much as possible, come for the entire weekend, but she had brought with her her lover—her first lover, in fact. They had met in college, lost each other for a while, and remet in graduate school. His name was Moon Mandelbaum. He was not only Jewish but certainly what her family thought of as dreadfully, horribly, "Sixties." He played the guitar, his hair was long, he defended the student revolts, was firmly counterculture, and, unlike her family, did not defend Mayor Daley for his behavior at the Democratic convention. Quite the contrary: he had been there, and had seen the police force demonstrators backward through plate glass windows; he was not happily accepted as a witness.

Moon did not own a dinner jacket, and he refused,

with Kate's encouragement, to don so much as a tie for the major event of the weekend, the announcement of her brother William's engagement to the woman both she and Moon had met for the first time on their arrival. Moon was pleasant, laid-back, as the phrase went, and likely to persuade anyone annoyed with him to mellow out, take it easy, not to get excited—phrases perfectly designed to arouse all available Fanslers to fury. He and Kate swam in the ocean, played desultory tennis, and disappeared for long periods to engage in what no one in the family could for a minute either doubt or comment on.

The atmosphere was, at the outset, seething, but then, as Kate told Moon, it always was at family get-togethers, at least since the death of the Fansler parents. At this weekend, however, she had Moon to cheer her on, and her favorite brother, the only brother she liked at all, to support. It neither began nor ended as a promising weekend for anyone but Kate and Moon.

The Fansler family, comprising aunts, uncles, and an amazing assortment of cousins, was impressive, as was the house—large enough for most of them; the others were at nearby inns. Moon was astonished at the numbers. His family consisted of his mother, father, grandfather, and himself. They were all that remained of a much larger number of Austrian kin. Moon, however, watching regret and the horror of memories filter through his grandfather and parents, emerged willing to be American, looking forward.

He had been given a violin early in life, but had in his early teens transferred his musical ability, which was considerable, to the guitar. That was about all Kate knew of his background, except that he prized literature and was determined to teach it, as she did herself.

The first Kate heard of a problem was from her hostess sister-in-law, who cornered Kate during cocktails and ordered her, in no uncertain terms, not only to befriend William's fiancée but to make her welcome. "Don't let William fill you with any of his nonsense," she had added. "Everyone gets cold feet at the thought of marriage, but no one pays the least attention to such things. I'm counting on you, Kate."

This was not very clever of Kate's sister-in-law since Kate, up to that moment, had had not the slightest idea that William was anything but happy. Now, of course, she felt called upon to seek him out and discover if there was real trouble, or only last minute qualms.

Kate was quite prepared to believe in the force of last minute qualms: she never intended to marry herself, and didn't altogether see why anyone else bothered either, unless they were overcome with the desire for little ones. (The first doubt Kate began to have about Moon was when he showed himself delighted to sport with her nieces and nephews; when Kate objected to his loving uncle act, he only laughed and deserted the smallest Fanslers to lead her off for a swim. Kate loved the ocean.)

William, when finally cornered in the billiard room

where he was playing by himself and looking anything but bridegroom-eager, agreed to a walk along the shore. It was evening, and the beach would be largely deserted. Kate removed her evening shoes and walked barefoot through the sand. William followed suit. They left their shoes on a rock and walked close to the incoming tide, wetting their feet and their clothes. Something in this brought back to William—or so Kate surmised to Moon—their old companionship. At any rate, he began to talk.

"Do you believe in the Oedipus complex?" he asked, to get himself going. "You know, the idea that one marries someone like one's mother."

" 'I want a girl just like the girl that married dear old Dad,' " Kate sang. "Is that what you mean?"

"That's what I'm worried about. Dear old Dad was a bastard, no doubt about that, but he might have been a bit better if he hadn't married Mother. I mean, alternate shrieking and sulking are hardly likely to turn a sourpuss sweet."

"Am I to gather that you suspect Muriel"—such was his fiancée's name—"of being like Mother, and if so, why did you ever agree to marry her?"

"That's just it, Puss." Without thinking, he reverted to what he had called her when they were children, since at Kate's birth it had been explained to him that he had been given a kitten and his mother had been given Kate. "I feel like a child all over again, watching a loved and loving mother turn into a horror. Well, you remember what she came to be like, when

169

she wasn't being the perfect lady. It wasn't many years after you were born that the transformation took place, now that I think of it."

"I daresay she hadn't been happy to find herself pregnant again. After all, her youngest boy was six, and you were eight. I should think it would be enough to turn anyone into a crank. Not, I should add, that I ever found any reason to excuse her or to like her. I guess she left me more alone than she did you boys, at least when you were young."

"You always seemed to slip out from under her pall. I envied you, in fact. Life was hell till we went away to boarding school."

A wave rose against them, and Kate pulled her skirts up belatedly. She wrung them out with a laugh, and pulled William farther inshore. "What are you trying to do?" she asked him. "If Muriel is like Mother, surely you must have noticed that before now."

"That's what's so odd; I didn't. I'm not in love with her, but I didn't expect to be. You remember the row over Deborah; I couldn't face anything like that again. Muriel is fun; she likes to ski and the rest of it; the family took to her; she's good-looking and she likes sex. She wanted to marry me, so why not? I know this all sounds a little cold-blooded, but I hadn't started to think of it in this way until recently. The last few weeks, in fact."

"Tell."

"Our engagement was a settled thing. This weekend was arranged. It wasn't to be announced until next week, but everyone who had the slightest interest in the matter knew. I thought she and I would be able to relax and enjoy this time, but suddenly she began being different. Altogether different—like Mother. What's the fancy word I'm looking for?"

"Transmogrified?"

"That's it—turned into a monster. It began over where we would live. I'd made up my mind that it wasn't going to be the East Side. I like the West Side. I like the people there, I like the feeling. I like Moon, by the way," he added, clarifying his feelings about the West Side. "New Yorkers are either East Side or West Side and I'm West Side. I thought she'd agreed. But dear older brother offered to get us an apartment in his exclusive building, and I said no. She had a fit. She sulked, she screamed, she walked out on me, she hung up on me, she behaved like a bitch."

"And?"

"I was clearly burned up when we got together, and she apologized and said it was some drugs she'd been taking for anxiety or cramps or something, and that she wasn't really like that. We let the matter of the apartment drop, but of course it came up again and I could see she wasn't going to give way. She wanted to live on the East Side. She wanted to live in an exclusive building."

"The sort Jackie Kennedy lives in. No Jews."

"Exactly. She was alternately sweet and angry. And damn it, Kate, I don't know how to get out of it now,

171

after this bloody weekend and all. We got into a fight last night over something to do with the wedding—never mind what, it doesn't matter—but suddenly I was back in the house where we grew up and Mother was screaming at me that I had to go join the Knickerbocker Grays, or whatever the hell they were called. I learned pretty quickly that life would be hell if I didn't do what she wanted. Can you believe it, I've got myself attached to a woman exactly like her? Can Freud have been right all along? Am I going crazy, Kate?"

"I've heard it said—don't ask me with what veracity—that we tend to marry people like our parents, because we've learned to deal with that. Maybe you got caught up in that syndrome. Maybe you were just misled. Anyone can put on an act for a while, until something jolts the person into his or her ordinary behavior. Hell, Will, I don't know what I'm talking about, but I do think that whatever the row, you can't marry someone you don't want to marry because everyone who's anyone knows you said you would."

"Do you think I could be wrong about her?"

"It doesn't seem like it."

"Would you mind talking with her, sounding her out, seeing what you think?"

"I'll talk to her if you want. I'll ask her to play tennis. Does she play tennis?"

William nodded. "She plays everything, very well."

"Okay, we'll play, we'll talk. But don't expect me to

see through her if she decides to beguile me. I'm not the Delphic oracle. I'm not even a Fansler, except in name. I've always suspected Mother of getting it on with the tutor or someone."

"We didn't have a tutor."

"I know. I'm thinking of the rumors about Edith Wharton's parentage—all nonsense, really. I'm just trying to convey the possibility that I may not be much help in figuring out what she's like. But if you want out, William, I'll be with you when the band begins to play."

He hugged her for a moment, and then they walked on in silence, Kate racking her brain as to what to talk about to Muriel.

As it turned out, while they volleyed the ball back and forth warming up for a game, Muriel did most of the talking. She exclaimed about the beauty of this house, the hospitality of the Fanslers, the fun of knowing such a family.

"Fun?" Kate had asked before she could stop herself.

"Oh, yes. They're all such warm, friendly people and have made me feel so welcome. Shall we toss for serve? Rough or smooth?"

"Rough," Kate said, she hoped not prophetically. It was smooth. Muriel chose to serve.

Kate was a fairly good tennis player, and the two found themselves evenly matched. The first set was three-three when Kate admitted to thirst, and they sat down together in a small pavilion beside the court and helped themselves to drinks from a refrigerator there. After all, Kate reminded herself, the point was not tennis, which she couldn't seem to keep her mind on anyway, but was rather to get to know Muriel.

"You find the Fanslers more comfortable to be with than I do, it seems," Kate said in what she hoped was a provocative manner.

"But they're all wonderful," Muriel said. "I know William has had his problems with them too, but I think it's always hard to get one's family into perspective, and I've offered to help him to get a better sense of proportion."

"Do you have your own family in perspective?" Kate asked. "If so, I envy you."

"It's an altogether different matter," Muriel said with some asperity. "My family was a mess. Not a bit like yours. Altogether *un*like yours."

Kate stared at her.

"My father drank, heavily," Muriel said, staring at her polished fingernails. "We all got away as soon as possible. My mother couldn't deal with him and was so afraid of offending him that we were on our own. An awful family, really, not at all like yours."

Kate could not think of a sensible answer to this, and offered none. They could hardly get into a slanging match about whose family was the worse mess. All that was clear was that Kate's family had had money and Muriel's had not. Kate tried to think generously: if she had never had enough money, would she not also find the Fanslers wonderfully agreeable? The question was, however, Kate reminded herself, whether Muriel was in love with William or with the Fansler family's social standing.

"I know what you're thinking," Muriel said, twirling her tennis racquet. "You're thinking I only want William for his money. Well, I admit, his money's a part of it. But I wouldn't marry anyone I didn't love just because he had money."

"But would you marry someone you did love who had no money?" Kate idly asked.

"Of course," Muriel said. "William's being lovable came first. Shall we go on with the game, or was it only an excuse to talk to me?"

"I did want to talk to you," Kate said. "But let's finish the game, by all means."

William came to Kate's room while she was changing for dinner. She had spent the remainder of the afternoon in her tennis clothes, wandering around and thinking. She had, in the course of this, been intercepted by Moon, and she had confided her problem to him. In the end she told him everything, including her instinctive dislike and distrust of Muriel, and William's fears.

"What's worrying me," she said to Moon, "is not that she's interested in his money. Why shouldn't she be? It's that I can't get over the feeling that's all she's interested in. Also, she isn't very smart. If she were,

175

she would have spoken to me differently—do you know what I mean, Moon?—she would have figured out the sort of person I was. It's clear she hasn't really listened to William, and can't believe that anyone lucky enough to be a Fansler wouldn't understand someone else's longing to be one too. I don't think she'll make William happy, but I hate making decisions for other people. Maybe I'm wrong. I don't know what to do."

Moon didn't know what to advise, but he did point out that William's was one of the oldest dilemmas and had therefore given rise to many of the oldest stories in the world: the rich man (or woman, of course) putting it about that he had no money to find out how true his lover's love was.

"Do you mean tell her William won't have any money? Why should she believe that? And anyway, she'd only have to check with my brothers and their wives, who quite like Muriel, to learn that it wasn't true."

"Let me think about it," Moon said. And they walked for a long time in silence while Moon thought. One of the things that Kate found enchanting about Moon was that you could hear him thinking—that is, could sense him thinking. However the perception occurred, one *felt* Moon thinking. In the end, reluctantly and tentatively, he offered an idea. An idea that Kate then offered to William when he came to her room.

"Do you like Moon?" Kate asked William.

"I do, actually. Very much. I doubt the family cares

for him. In fact, they're being just this side of rude. Why did we have to be born into such a family, Kate?"

"Well, at least our father didn't drink, like Muriel's."

"Drink? Muriel's father? Don't be silly. I've met the poor chap. I don't think he's been let off the leash long enough to have a drink. What on earth gave you the idea that he drank?"

"Never mind that. Look, William, do you think you could play a role?"

William looked blank. "A role? What on earth do you mean?"

"Oh, dear," Kate said. "Moon had an idea. See what you think. In the next day or so, spend a lot of time with Moon. He's ready whenever you are. Then tell Muriel that Moon has convinced you that the rich life is not a good one, that Jesus said to sell all you have and give the money to the poor, that you want to live the simple life with Moon in a sort of commune—well, I know, this does sound mad, but people are thinking that way these days. You'll have to make it sound believable. Pretend you expect her to join you joyously in this. Say you're keeping some money back for an annuity that will support you in your old age, but for now you want to make it on your own. Hell, I don't know, William. Try it."

William, who had been sitting on Kate's bed, flopped backward. There was a long silence. "Is Moon willing to tutor me in this, so to speak? To give me the right lingo and all that?"

"Of course. But remember, if she says she wants to stay with you no matter what, you're stuck."

"Kate, I said she was like Mother; I didn't say she was after my money."

"I know. But I don't know if she really loves you. All we do know is that she gets into an uproar when you seem to withhold the goodies like an apartment near the rest of the family. If it's you she wants, and since you thought you loved her, you'll have to try to make it work. Of course," Kate added, "don't feel pushed to do this. It's just a suggestion, and not a terrifically brilliant or original one at that."

For the rest of that evening, and most of the next day, William hung around with Moon. He seemed to be avoiding Muriel, which lent credence to his new-found affection for and allegiance to Moon, as well as his need for encouragement to tell her about his decision to follow Moon into a commune. Kate knew that Moon would never dream of joining a commune, and she hoped Muriel wouldn't get a chance to ask him straight out, because Moon, Kate knew, would not lie.

Moon must have had some powerful effect upon William, however, because he went on with the plan and held to it even in the face of his whole furious family. Muriel had gone running to them, and they had descended on poor William, who, however, was certainly old enough to decide what to do with his life and bold enough to tell them he felt entitled to make

178

up his own mind. Muriel had a fit, she screamed, she carried on, but in the end they had to cancel the engagement party and Muriel left. The family tried to assure her that William would change his mind, but William remained adamant, and in the end he left with Kate and Moon, having failed, however, to retrieve from Muriel the rather large diamond engagement ring he had given her. Not that he tried hard.

"She's entitled to it," he told Kate. "I feel that I've behaved very badly, but oh, Kate my dear, what an escape. *What* an escape."

Eventually William married someone else, suitable, pleasant, but hardly exciting. She was a good mother, however, and Kate was fond of their children. The whole episode of that summer retreated in Kate's mind, not to say was actually repressed, because she felt rather ashamed of herself. She and Moon went their different ways shortly after, as a result of their having taken part in that charade, and Kate, in fact, as she now reflected, was not to meet up in any meaningful way with Moon until many, many years later, at, of all places, Harvard. And at that time, meeting unexpectedly, neither of them had even thought of, let alone mentioned, what Kate now dubbed the Muriel episode, the shameful—well, it was shameful, really—Muriel episode.

Kate lifted herself off the couch, threw aside the pillow that had stood in for Banny, and went to phone Leslie with her news of a recovered memory.

But why, she wondered, as the phone rang, had thinking of Banny helped that memory to return?

And then it came to her: Moon had had a dog that summer, not a Saint Bernard, but a large, fluffy, friendly dog who went with them everywhere and had been loved by everyone, though by the older Fanslers with moderation. Rather to Kate's surprise, the dog had been especially fond of Muriel, and Muriel of the dog. Rack her brain though she might, Kate could not remember the dog's name. But it seemed to Kate that the mutual affection between Muriel and the dog had made Moon the least bit unhappy about taking part in Muriel's deception. Still, Moon did not believe that anyone should marry anyone, and certainly not if one of them didn't want to.

"Hello, Leslie," Kate said into the phone. "I think I've got it. Hold everything. I'm coming over. I think I'll ask Reed to join us there later, if that's all right with you."

Thirteen

Hours later, Kate, Reed, Leslie, and Jane were still discussing the situation, over a meal of Chinese takeout, and for about the eleventh time they rehearsed the ever more demanding and far-reaching questions.

"You're quite sure you didn't make this whole thing up?" Jane, who considered herself the most practical member of the gathering, asked Kate. Reed, no question, was also practical, but when it came to Kate, Jane did not consider him as entirely objective as he could be expected to be in other circumstances.

"Of course I didn't," Kate said, between mouthfuls of fried dumpling. "I know it seems improbable that she should have fallen for it, but there were two factors on our side—that is, William's side. One was that

181

she had clearly overestimated Fansler loyalty to her. They were prepared to accept her as better in every way than others William might have dragged home, but they weren't devoted to her enough to discount the possibility that she may have been after William's money. Wasn't everyone after the Fansler money? Also, thinking about it now, I realize that the fact that I was there with Moon softened the family up, so to speak. I always brought out their most confrontational side, and they were so horrified by Moon they were quite willing to believe he and I might magically have managed between us to bewitch poor, dear William."

"We are, therefore," Leslie announced, in the crisp tones of one trying to wrap up a lengthy meeting, "agreed that Muriel has been seething all these years and has finally taken her revenge in the way we know. Are we agreed?"

"It's a possibility," Reed said, as he and Kate plunged into the moo-shu pork. "But a possibility based on a number of assumptions. You accept the first assumption and then the second, and before you know it you have a whole theory that hangs together beautifully if you manage to forget that you haven't a shred of evidence for the first assumption, the basis of the whole thing. There's no getting away from that. On the other hand, if we agree, as we seem to have, that this is an act of revenge against Kate, and if this is the only source of deep resentment against her that Kate can come up with, I think we might as well pursue it, at least for a time. If we cannot locate Muriel, we'll have to send Kate into psychoanalysis for a more thorough dredging into her past." He smiled at Kate, who, he knew, thought as little of classical psycho-analysis as he did.

"So," Leslie observed, "the question of *Who is Muriel, what is she?* remains the operative one."

"Perhaps William knows what became of her," Jane suggested. "One does somehow often manage to hear about one's discarded loves, at least in a general sort of way."

"Not likely," Kate said. "William has not got any less stuffy with the years. He's got grown children and works on Wall Street. He probably doesn't even remember who Muriel was. I mean, let's face it, if I repressed this sorry episode, William has probably banished it to oblivion."

"You remembered it," Leslie said, "because you have a lot of guilt attached to it. I doubt that William does, though I agree with Jane that you ought to ask him, just in case he has some news of her. I mean, if she's been dead for decades, we're clearly whistling in a wind tunnel. But the salient point, as far as I can see"—and Leslie put down her chopsticks in a deter-mined way—"is whether Muriel knew, or surmised, or guessed that Kate was in back of her rejection by the Fanslers. Can you know, Kate, that Muriel blamed you, or is there a possibility she didn't and thus cannot be considered in the present circumstances?"

"Good point," Kate said. "But I'm really sure she knew it was me behind it; in fact I remember, now, that she told me so. I'd forgotten that part. The row about her was still going on when Moon and I left. She came up to us as we were getting into the car to go. She paid no attention to Moon, and it was his supposed commune, after all, that William was supposed to be going to join. She just stood there, facing me, and said, 'I guess you're feeling satisfied with yourself, you stuck-up bitch,' or similar words. And she spat at me and stalked off. I remember now; Moon took out the bottom of his T-shirt and wiped the spit off my face. I'd forgotten that part."

Absolute quiet greeted this memory. Kate looked shaken.

"I still think Kate should have a chat with William about Muriel," Jane said into the silence. And Kate agreed to that.

They began to gather up the cartons of food. It seemed settled, without the matter being mentioned, that questions of who Muriel was and where she was would be deferred until tomorrow.

But when Kate had enticed her brother William into meeting her for a drink the next day, he turned out to have no idea what had become of Muriel. William had been worried about meeting Kate, supposing, as her brothers always did if she asked to see them, that she would request either money or, what they dreaded slightly more, financial advice. Their relief when the subject turned out to have nothing to do with money was always so great that they quite agreeably discussed whatever was on her mind. (Kate's brothers, although she neither knew nor guessed it, secretly agreed with her that their wayward sister was not their father's daughter but the offspring of some belated and, in fact, quite uncharacteristic fling of her mother's. The sexual mores of the Nineties had made such a thought about one's mother rather more romantic than scurrilous.) But about Muriel, William knew nothing.

Indeed, he recalled the episode only vaguely and reluctantly. "You should have simply persuaded me to tell her to go to hell," he said now. Kate, with great restraint, did not challenge this extraordinary statement.

"You have no idea what became of her?" Kate persisted.

"No. She sent me an invitation to her wedding. I do remember that. Of course, I threw it away before Patricia could ask who she was." Patricia was William's wife. "It was years ago at any rate. Why on earth do you want to know about Muriel? Well forgotten, I should have thought. Are you writing your memoirs, God forbid?"

"No," Kate assured him. "I just happened to remember her the other day and I got to wondering. You don't remember her married name?"

"I don't even remember her maiden name. That was thirty years ago, Kate, and she wasn't exactly in the first flush of youth then. She might be sixty now. I wish you'd tell me what this is all about."

Kate did not tell him, and she let the conversation drift in other directions. But as William was preparing to pay the bill he suddenly stopped, having thought of something. "I've just remembered," he said. "Funny how memories come back like that, all of a sudden. I remember the last thing she said to me. I tried to be at least polite as she was getting ready to leave but she wasn't having any of it. Well, I said, good luck anyway, or something equally foolish, and then she sort of snorted and said: 'I bet your sister never marries, but if she does, I'm sorry for the guy. Very sorry.'"

"And what did you make of that?" Kate asked.

"What's to make of it? I thought she was sorry for any man who married you. Sorry, dear, but that's what I thought, and you did ask for every last memory. What else could she have meant?"

"I'm sure that's exactly what she meant," Kate said. They were by now outside on the sidewalk and Kate kissed William goodbye in a sisterly way and walked off in the opposite direction from him.

That evening, when Kate and Reed were both home from work and winding down, drink in hand and feet up, the telephone rang and Reed went to answer it.

Kate could tell from the look on his face when he returned that the news was bad.

"Toni has died," he said. "That was Harriet. The police have asked to interview her. She's down at the first precinct. I'll be with her during the interview, unless she prefers to talk with them alone."

"But I thought Toni was getting better—had come out of the coma and all," Kate wailed.

"There was another clot. That's all Harriet had time to say. I don't think Harriet's in real danger, but I'd better get over there."

"I'll come too."

"Better not. The police get fussy in these cases, and it may look as though we're ganging up on them."

"We *are* ganging up on them. Will they let her out when they're through interviewing her?"

"Of course. They've no reason to keep her. There's no evidence against her, and no probable cause. They're fishing. Anyway, they always like to question those nearest to the victim, which is usually family but also business associates. What I have to do is get her a lawyer. I know a good one I hope I can persuade to take this on."

"Can't you be her lawyer?"

"Not a good idea. I'll consult, of course." Reed was looking for his coat.

"I'm still coming," Kate said. "I just want her to know I'm there, even if I have to wait outside on a bench or wherever."

Reed shrugged, helped her into her coat, and they were off. Kate, thrown back in the taxi, realized that she was far more worried about Harriet than about Toni.

Toni was dead. Surely one should feel more sorrow for the dead. But Harriet meant a great deal to Kate, and the thought of her being convicted of murder could not be contemplated. What Kate felt was profound regret that Toni had ever got mixed up in this case, that she had ever allowed Harriet to bring Toni in. Kate had always, she now had to realize, felt deep reservations about Toni. But she was young, and dead, and would be mourned when Harriet was out of danger. Those thoughts, Kate knew, were harsh, and she did not intend to share them with anyone. Reed, she felt certain, would have guessed in any case.

As Reed had suspected, she was not allowed to go with him to see Harriet. Indeed, she sat, as she had anticipated, on a chair and waited. But Reed would tell Harriet that she, Kate, had come with him, and that was the important thing.

Reed emerged a relatively short time later. "I think she's holding up," he said, "though very upset about Toni's death, for which, being Harriet, she naturally blames herself. I tried to shock her into understanding that she was the one who needs all of our efforts now, including her efforts; Toni was beyond our help. When people are in a state like Harriet's, you have to say the simplest things and keep repeating them. I told her she would have a lawyer tomorrow, with whom she could discuss the whole matter, and that they certainly wouldn't hold her. She was babbling on about bail. I do often wonder at how little citizens, even private eyes, know about the penal law. Do you, Kate, know how long people can be kept after arrest?"

"Of course not," Kate said.

"Six days, or one hundred and forty-four hours. I told her you had come with me, and that neither of us believed for a minute that she had killed Toni. Harriet is as bad as you; she didn't seem to know that she was not being arrested, let alone that had she been, she would have been arraigned and then remanded without bail, which is set at a later date before a judge. I do find it a bit appalling that two of the most intelligent women I know are so ignorant of law."

"Is that the truth?" Kate said. "I supposed it's because we don't expect to find ourselves in the hands of the police, and if we should, we would be able to hire a lawyer. Self-satisfaction leading to inexcusable ignorance, not to put too fine a point on it."

They rode for a while in silence in the taxi taking them home, where Reed would make his call to the lawyer he hoped would take on Harriet's case. "Do you really not believe for a minute that Harriet killed Toni?" Kate asked, after a time.

189

"I can imagine Harriet learning something about Toni she didn't like, for instance, and resigning from the partnership in a huff, slamming the door behind her. I can't see her hitting Toni, or anybody else, over the head with a blunt instrument. But I suspect there may be more than she's told us about what she and Toni found out. You do realize, Kate, that Toni may have been killed because she was close to learning who was behind our little drama. And she may have told Harriet, or she may not."

"Can you find out from Harriet?"

"I certainly hope so, if she is willing to be frank with us about Toni and their partnership, including its clients. She'll be expecting us to question her, you can be sure of that. You know, Kate," he went on, "I'm beginning to realize that I never much liked Toni and I've never stopped to face that fact or to ask myself why."

"You mean, we should be sorrier than we are?"

"Well, sorrier in a more personal way. Death is always shocking and frightful, but some deaths rock us more than others. Had Harriet died . . ."

"I know what you mean. And Toni was young, which makes it worse. I realize I took it altogether for granted that she would recover, once she was out of the coma."

"I don't know that anyone can ever be said to have wholly recovered from traumatic head wounds. They lie in wait sometimes, those kinds of traumas." He took Kate's hand, and they rode the rest of the way in silence.

In the end, it took several days for Reed to persuade the lawyer he wanted for Harriet to take the case. The man had a very overcrowded calendar. "As all successful defense lawyers do, don't they?" Kate commented. "Either they're too busy or no one wants them—the way of the world." Reed and Kate had agreed to meet the lawyer's fees. Harriet, of course, objected, saying she preferred to settle for someone assigned by the court. Reed pointed out that such a lawyer might be first-rate, but also might not, and that he and Kate would feel better with a known quantity of law experience on Harriet's side.

"I'll pay you back if it takes the rest of my life," Harriet warned them.

"Of course you will," Reed said. "If you don't, we'll take it out in labor. Let's concentrate on what's facing us at the moment."

And so they sat together one evening to discuss the case: Archie Press, Harriet's lawyer, Harriet, Kate, and Reed. Reed's point, which he had persuaded Archie and Harriet at least to sit still for, was that they must prove that Harriet could not have committed the crime and that there was no probable cause the police could offer.

"It would help," Archie pointed out, "if we could find the real murderer, if any."

"Well," Kate said, "she didn't hit herself over the head."

"Sorry," Archie agreed. "I mean a murderer as opposed to a casual lunatic who happened into the office and decided that Toni was his enemy. That does, alas, happen in New York. You all read the papers, so I don't have to offer examples."

"Don't they leave evidence most of the time?"

"No. Usually they are caught for one crime and end up confessing to the others. We're speaking here of killers who know nothing of their victims who are unfortunate enough to get in the killer's way, cross his path, be there when he wants to steal something."

"And you think it would be hard to prove it was that kind of killing?" Kate asked.

"Hard to impossible. We have only two hopes. Of course we shall maintain Harriet didn't do it; that is the path I suggest. One hope is that you discover who did, and that the murderer has some connection with the victim. That is the path I gather Harriet suggests. I think it's worth following, but I'm going to have to leave that to the rest of you, unless you can offer me more than we have now. Our best hope at the moment," Archie added, "lies in the papers in Toni's office. They may turn out to be worthless, or they may already have been removed. The police locked off the premises, but they have to give me access. There may be something there that will lead us to the culprit. But I'm not betting on it."

"You don't sound very optimistic," Harriet said, in the tone of one noticing the weather.

"It's not my job to be optimistic," Archie replied. "Let's look at the facts, ignoring for the moment whatever evidence the papers in the office may provide. You had every opportunity to commit the crime. We can't find the woman you met in the bathroom, although we're trying. I've hired someone to follow up every lead from every office on that floor, but we've gotten nowhere. You had the key to the office door, which was locked and opened with a key. The police have no case as yet, but I can't say I exactly like our situation."

"Toni could have opened it from the inside to the visitor, whom she may have known," Harriet said.

"True enough. Her fingerprints are on the door, naturally. But did she then just turn her back on the visitor, offering her head for a violent attack?"

"She might easily have turned away if it was someone she knew, or even if it wasn't," Kate insisted. "We don't expect everyone who comes into our office to be planning mayhem. Whoever it was hit her and departed, taking the weapon with her or him."

"Maybe," Archie allowed. "At least I think we're agreed in theory that Toni knew whoever it was who hit her, probably knew her well. Or him," he added a bit belatedly.

"Why do we all think it's a woman?" Kate asked. "I know I do."

"It's something about the way it happened," Reed

193

said. "Toni would almost certainly have been more suspicious of a man, even if she knew him. We've learned enough of her life to know there was no man in it at the moment, no lover or other male attachment around. Harriet is pretty sure of that, and the police haven't been able to uncover anyone at all likely. Also, and I know this sounds as though I'm pushing it," Reed said, "but somehow I can't see a man hitting her in quite that way. I know that's not very persuasive. It's just an impression."

"And one which we all share," Harriet agreed.

"Here's what I suggest," Reed said, nodding at Archie to indicate they had already discussed these suggestions. "I think that Kate, with Harriet's help, should try to locate Muriel. Kate will tell you who Muriel is," he added for Harriet's benefit. "Archie and I will go over the papers left in the office, and arrange for some private detectives to follow up certain leads."

"Don't you think I could be a help with the papers?" Harriet asked. "I was her partner."

"We'll consult you if we need to," Reed said. "Those papers will be documents available to the prosecution and the defense, and Archie had better deal with them in a formal way. You and Kate work from the other end. Kate might start with the right-wing characters we originally suspected; they might lead us somewhere. Harriet could try to track down Muriel. Or vice versa. Are we all set, then?"

Archie nodded. Kate and Harriet looked at him,

their vague uncertainty about the paths ahead evident. "Good," Reed said, "let's drink to that." And he went off to get the fixings.

Later, when Harriet and Archie had gone, Kate again asked Reed if he was entirely convinced of Harriet's innocence and really thought her working with Kate was a good idea.

"Aren't *you* entirely convinced?"

"I asked you first."

"I think I'm convinced, as you probably are, ninety-nine percent. If we're wrong, you may pick up a clue to why we're wrong if you work closely with her. I haven't any fear of her doing you harm; I hope you haven't. Because if you do, then we'd better make other arrangements."

"No fear," Kate said. "I'm just damn uneasy about the whole thing."

"Which is simply a sign of intelligence," Reed said.

"I wish Toni hadn't died."

"I too," Reed said. "Dying made it murder."

"In the first degree, I suppose," Kate said, trying to sound intelligent about the law.

"No. Murder one since October 1995 is murder for hire or murder with torture and other defined atrocities. Sorry to have berated you for not knowing the penal law. Why on earth should you? Let's go to bed; I'm bushed. Murder will always do that to you."

"I wonder how Banny is," Kate said. Reed, still a bit tetchy, responded by pleading with her not to mention that damn dog, whom he missed too, damn it.

"And we only had the beast for a few days, at least I did. We're being foolish."

"Always a good sign," Kate assured him.

Fourteen

THE next day, Monday, was the start of Kate's weeklong spring break. This holiday always occurred in the exact middle of the spring term, bearing no relation either to Easter or to the vernal equinox, but it was always welcome as the only break in a long semester. Kate determined that by the time of her return to classes she would either have found Muriel or eliminated her as a possibility. Harriet and Kate sat together in Kate's study and Kate reiterated Leslie's idea about an ancient grudge (assumed ancient because Kate did not remember it) and then explained about Muriel and all the memory searching that had resulted in her identification, if identification it could be called.

Harriet took this all in, demonstrating her habit of

listening intently when she was being offered information. She was quiet for a time.

"The problem," she eventually said, "as of course you've already seen, is that whoever Muriel is now, she has not shown herself in this investigation. Either we know nothing of her, or we must surmise her from the people we do have. There is no way, for instance, that Dorothy Hedge could be Muriel, because you'd surely have recognized her even after all these years."

"I suppose I would have," Kate said dubiously. "Yet, when I talked to Dorothy, I wasn't thinking of Muriel or the past in any way."

"No, but you had your antennae out, so to speak. Anything the least bit noticeable would have been noticed."

"Let's assume that, for the moment, at least. I suggest that we go back to the right-wing group idea, and look for whoever is behind that, with the advantage that we are assuming for the moment that *whoever* is Muriel. I take it you met the mother of the bad boy who wrote the letter. Could she have been Muriel?"

"Good heavens, Kate, how the hell would I know?"

"By her age, for one thing."

"Exactly. Your brother pointed out that Muriel might well be sixty by now. Right-wing Mama could be sixty. She looked a bit older, I thought, but who can tell? What you've got to do is get the university's records on her son, which should give you some background. Get hold of his application to the university if you can. Meanwhile, I think I'll go visit her again, let her argue me into joining her reactionary group."

"She might know you've been questioned about the murder."

"She probably won't, but if she does that will tell us something about how closely she's following all this. It will also give me a chance to say how rotten our government and police are."

"What it comes down to," Kate sighed, "is that we have to go back to the very beginning."

"Always a good idea," Harriet said. "I do hope," she added after a pause, "that you aren't harboring even the slightest suspicion that I attacked Toni. Not that that would keep me from this investigation, since anything I find out will only go to prove my innocence. But I just thought I would ask."

"I'm not harboring the slightest suspicion," Kate said. "The big question as far as I'm concerned is, can we assume that whoever killed her was connected to our investigation? If it was someone from her earlier life or from another case, that makes me more worried about proving your innocence."

"I've considered that. But I don't really think that Toni had any cases I didn't know about, and none of the ones I know about are the least likely to have led to murder, least of all hers. Not that she wasn't secretive about some things. There were certainly arrangements she made that she didn't discuss in my presence or where I could overhear. But I always assumed these had to do with her private life. It doesn't make sense that they had to do with a case; we discussed all our cases all the time, and anyway, yours was our main job at the moment."

"But the police, according to Archie, haven't found any indication that she had a private life, at least not a complicated one at all or one likely to lead to violence. You certainly didn't think she did."

"No. But I almost never went to her house. We didn't have a social life together—you know, drinks, walks, meals with conversation. Ours was strictly a business arrangement. Now that I think of it, perhaps that is a little odd. But I'm such a loner myself that it didn't really occur to me to think anything of it. You know, Kate, you're the only person I've let get close to me in years, and that was partly because I like you, and partly because you helped me out in a very serious personal matter."

"I do wish," Kate said, "that everything we dredged up didn't lead to a dead end."

"Well, on to our assigned task then," Harriet said, rising. "Me to Mama, you to son's records. Let's talk tonight in case either of us has discovered anything at all."

Kate had a harder time of it than she had expected. The English department, she knew, had records, but the Bad Boy, as she and Harriet had taken to calling him, was not a student in the English department.

That meant accosting the Dean's secretary and demanding a student's record. This Kate did, at first in her most tactful manner, then with a bit more authority as the Dean's secretary held firmly to her instructions that no student's file was to be given out except with the Dean's written instruction, and the Dean had taken himself off to the Bahamas for the spring break, exact whereabouts unknown, or so the secretary claimed. Only after Kate had tracked down the Associate Dean, who was at home nursing a cold, did she manage to wrench the records from the diligent secretary.

"I was just following orders," the secretary said rather apologetically, handing over the records. "You will look at them here, won't you?"

"Of course I will, and you acted correctly," Kate said, also conciliatory.

Bad Boy's records were more revealing than Kate had dared to hope. He had applied several times to the university and been turned down. He was at last accepted upon the recommendation of one of the university's major donors, a man Kate recognized as a member of a foundation subsidizing right-wing publications and organizations on many campuses. (This identification of the donor was not of course in the application; Kate had long known of him, as had many others who regretted the powerful financial influence of right-wing foundations on campus life.)

Bad Boy's folder also recorded his failure in several courses and his having been brought up on charges of plagiarism and cheating. He had not, however, been expelled—for reasons anyone might presume to guess. He had at least been warned that the offenses must not be repeated. Kate found it of interest that his ill-advised letter to the student newspaper had been included in his folder. His parents' names were, of course, given in his original application: father dead; mother a native and resident of Georgia, now living in New York, supposedly to be near her son. Bad Boy's original application had included a picture. He was not bad looking, except for a smirk on his face which appeared to be permanent. His name, Kate noted, was Kenneth Lawrence Thomas. His mother's name was Electra Thomas, a wonderfully appropriate name, whether she had been endowed with it at birth or had adopted it because she acted too wholly in defense of the father and patriarchal rights.

Kate was not surprised to discover, in reading over Bad Boy's (for so she continued to think of him, "Kenneth Lawrence" denoting nothing of special interest) transcript, that he had taken only the required courses in literature and that it was in these, she had no doubt, he had attempted to get away with plagiarism. Plagiarism was a plague these days among undergraduates, and Kate had always been astonished to discover the ineptitude of most plagiarists. One student had actually copied his paper from the introduction to the text used in class. Then there were the firms that wrote papers to order.

Kate dragged her wandering mind back to a contemplation of this particular student. The only other significant fact was that Bad Boy belonged to a fraternity that had years before become notorious for screaming epithets at some black students, thereby starting a riot. The fraternity's defense, Kate remembered, had been that its members had only observed that blacks had kinky hair, which was a simple matter of fact. Why should blacks be so sensitive about having their hair described for them? This was all very intriguing, but hardly suggested a connection to Muriel of long ago. Not at all certain what she had discovered, or what use it would be, Kate thanked the secretary politely, returned the folder, and went home to await Harriet. She hoped Harriet had discovered something more relevant, or at least surprising.

Harriet, upon her return, was, unlike Kate, to be seen as figuratively licking her lips. Electra could not be Muriel, Harriet assured Kate. Her Southern accent was real, and she was the mother of Dorothy Hedge and a still older sister, which made her far more advanced in years than Muriel could possibly be. "But I did discover a few delicious bits," Harriet assured Kate. "I deserve a single malt Scotch, as I'm sure you will agree."

Kate went to get it, returning to insist upon an immediate account.

"Well," Harriet said, this time licking her lips literally in appreciation of the Scotch, "just for starters, daughter Dorothy Hedge is not a renegade from the family's political positions. Quite the contrary. Mama was quite willing, upon being assured of my fervent agreement with all her opinions, and not knowing that I had any connection with you, to brag about how daughter Dorothy had fooled you into giving an account of your husband's kidnapping."

"Are you suggesting that the Hedge woman is Muriel?"

"Of course not, Kate. Do try to concentrate. You told me yourself that Muriel was not from the South, apart from all other considerations. No, the point is, dear Dorothy knew of the plot, aided and abetted it, and cheered it on. She lied to you, and induced you, with your unsophisticated sense of trust, to confide in her."

"I'm going to ignore that comment. I didn't lose a thing by *confiding* in her, as you put it. If I hadn't, you might not have rumbled to her true convictions—if Mama was telling you the truth, which can never be assumed."

"I'm ahead of you there. I believe nothing from the mouth of that woman without other evidence. Which I'm hoping Reed with his connections can get."

"What sort of evidence?"

"Mama said"—Harriet held out her glass for a refill—"that Dorothy came in to see Mama and Bad Boy at least once a week. If she comes in that often, she probably has an E-ZPass. If she has an E-ZPass, it records every time she goes through the tollbooths at the Henry Hudson Bridge."

"What you no doubt mean," Kate said with some acerbity, "is that her car went through the tollbooths. The identity of the driver is not revealed in the record, is it?"

"Rant on. It's evidence enough for me, if we can get it. I daresay E-ZPass's habit of sending a printed account each month must embarrass not a few wayward folks who have said they were going to be somewhere else at the time. However, that's not our case at the moment."

"Okay, what else did you learn?"

"Well, obviously that Mama and Bad Boy were connected to Reed's kidnapping. I know we guessed that, but now we know it. Unfortunately, it still doesn't tell us who was behind the whole scheme, and I admit I couldn't extract that from Mama in this visit even if she knows—and I'm not sure she does."

"She must know, if she agreed to take part and to let her son take part."

"Not necessarily. She could know who got in touch with her, but that person may not be the chief operator."

"Really, Harriet, you're beginning to sound as though we're dealing with the Mafia."

"And so I should. The analogy is not in the least farfetched. Think about it."

Kate, obeying this command, thought. After a time she said, "Harriet, who suggested the idea of using Banny to pass messages between us? Where did the idea come from?"

"Toni, of course. She said she'd used that method of communication before on a case."

"And who located Banny as the particular dog to be used as a go-between?"

"Toni did. She said she'd decided that Saint Bernard puppies were the most madly appealing puppies in the world, so she looked up some index of kennels and found one that bred Saint Bernards."

"And the person who bred them happened to know Dorothy Hedge who happens to be the daughter of Mama and the sister of Bad Boy. Quite a coincidence!"

"Not really. People around here who breed dogs live relatively nearby, in Connecticut or upstate, and naturally a breeder would know a woman who boards dogs. Toni found Banny through an ad. She told me all about it."

"Did she show you the ad?"

"Yes, she did, as a matter of fact. It said Saint Bernard puppies, with pedigrees, born on such and such a day—the usual thing, or so I supposed, in an ad for dogs."

"I see," Kate said. "Well, I'm going to have to figure it out when I have the time. Everybody seems so interconnected, and yet it can all be rationally explained. I'll ask Reed to see if he can get hold of the record of Dorothy's trips into Manhattan, or at least the trips her car took."

And with that their consultation ended, Harriet promising to visit Mama again and to try to work the conversation around to Reed's kidnapping and the details thereof.

That evening, Reed and Kate were joined by Archie. Each had something to report. None of it was major, but all of it at least, as Reed noted, left them with the impression that they were getting somewhere. Reed had managed, as it turned out with only small effort, to learn that Dorothy Hedge had indeed come to Manhattan regularly—and, most significantly, on the day that Toni was attacked. Upon being corrected by Kate, Reed admitted that all he could accurately testify to was that Dorothy's car had crossed the Henry Hudson Bridge on certain days and at certain hours. He also knew which toll lane she had entered, but that information, which he offered to Kate with a certain air of thoroughness, hardly signified. Kate stuck her tongue out at him.

Archie's news, following Reed's (which had followed Kate's account of Bad Boy's record and what Harriet had reported about Mama), was, if not riveting, certainly clarifying. He had obtained the result of police investigations in Toni's office as well as in her home, a studio in the East Village. Neither place had yielded startling results, although Archie had been pleased to learn that Toni's bank account had had a number of rather large deposits for which no source could be ascertained.

"Meaning?" Kate asked.

"Meaning that Toni or someone else made regular cash deposits into her account."

"How did you find out?"

"Kate, my dear," Archie said, as Reed had so often done, "your naïveté is charming. There is nothing in this age of computers anyone with a small degree of access and a knowledge of programs cannot discover. Anyway, the police found out at my suggestion, as it happened. Not that all this tells us much except that Toni was being paid for something neither she nor the payer wanted a record of. Also, and most important, the payments stopped after the attack."

"I should think that would be obvious."

"Perhaps to you." Archie smiled. "Us more tedious types like to remember about coincidence and other contingencies, such as, for example, that Toni was collecting the amounts in person and couldn't after the attacks, even if she was not attacked by the person who provided the money."

"Unlikely," Kate said.

"Perhaps."

"Are you, therefore, combining all our discoveries, assuming that Dorothy Hedge attacked Toni?" Kate asked.

"It seems possible. Getting to her bank account was a little harder—"

"Really, Archie," Kate said, "you make me wonder if there is any privacy left anywhere."

"Save your wonder for better things. There is no privacy if anybody really wants to find out. The point,

Kate," Archie said, "is that people like us lead such open lives that we need not worry about privacy. Although some underhanded people are surprisingly careless. I had a client whose wife was divorcing him. He had met his ladylove in a hotel and paid by credit card. That would not have mattered, since he paid the credit card bills, with which he troubled his wife only if her charges were lamentably out of line. In this case, however, he left the credit card at the hotel desk, and the assistant manager kindly telephoned his home to tell him. His wife was at home and took the call."

"He sounds like a particularly stupid assistant manager," Reed said. "I doubt he will go far."

"The really stupid one was my client. Lust draws blood from the brain. But getting back to this case, let me report that no sums comparable to those paid into Toni's account were withdrawn from Dorothy Hedge's."

"She might have kept a large stash of cash," Kate said. "Although I did notice that someone who came to pick up a dog while I was there paid with a check, if that means anything."

"Everything may mean something if we can only figure out what," Reed noted gloomily.

"We do know," Kate said to comfort him, "that Dorothy could have attacked Toni; that someone, probably not Dorothy, was paying Toni for something; that Dorothy lied to me; and that Mama and

Bad Boy are very nasty people indeed. Is there anything else?"

"Not much," Reed said, in his pleasantest voice, "except who dreamed up the kidnapping scheme, why was Toni attacked, and who is behind the whole thing and why."

"Don't worry," Archie said. "At least we can suggest that the Hedge woman had a motive, and a connection with a right-wing movement, which should let Harriet off from much more suspicion."

"Did his wife divorce him?" Kate asked.

Archie looked blank.

"The chap with the abandoned credit card."

"Oh, no. Finally she settled for a fair share of his stock options. They both figured out it was cheaper in the long run to stay together."

"What frightful clients you have."

"That's why Reed could talk me into defending Harriet. All she was accused of was murder, and probably only manslaughter at that."

Fifteen

THE next afternoon Reed was sitting at home listening to Bach and trying to organize the notes for a talk he had agreed to give in the spring at a time when the spring had seemed very far away. His thoughts were interrupted by the ringing of the house phone. He had to go into the pantry to answer it, wondering what on earth it could be. The doorman informed him that a Ms. Furst would like to come up. "Send her up," Reed said, and went to the door to wait for her.

"Well, Harriet, if you've come to see Kate she's not here. Gone to see a man about a dog—well, a person about a dog is what she said. That was absolutely all the information I was offered. Have you given up using the telephone?"

"Sorry to bother you," Harriet said. Reed invited her to sit down in the living room, but she declined the offer. "I wanted to see Kate's face when I told her," she explained. "I can't think why she isn't here."

"Told her what?" Reed asked, "or am I not to hear it until she does?"

"Perhaps I will sit down after all," Harriet said, taking a seat in the foyer and thus indicating her intention of not staying long. Reed remained standing, his posture displaying modified curiosity.

"I found the baseball bat," Harriet said.

"The baseball bat?"

"Reed," Harriet said, rising to her feet, "you know I admire Kate—as Jonson said of Shakespeare—'this side idolatry'; but I find her habit of repeating what one says extremely trying and I do wish you wouldn't also take it up."

"Sorry. What baseball bat?"

"The one that probably killed Toni, of course. I thought you had been paying attention to this case, Reed."

"So I have. But the baseball bat was only a supposition, an impulsive guess. Where did you find it and why do you think . . . ?"

"I found it in the room occupied by Bad Boy when he stays with Mama. She and I have become buddies, both of us supporting, as we do, the National Rifle Association, the bombing of abortion clinics, the death penalty, and the abolition of compassion as a government policy competing with growth. She
212

left me alone to consult with someone at the door and I poked around in my usual fashion. The bat was in the closet of his room and had clearly been washed, but I suspect a crime laboratory could make it speak nonetheless."

"Did you take it away?"

"I could hardly do that. I thought you might get the police or someone else to get a warrant or whatever it is you do when you think there is evidence. I think there is evidence that Bad Boy hit Toni over the head with the bat. Surely it's worth investigating."

"Surely it is," Reed said. "But it seems strange. I can't see Toni turning her back on a young man she didn't know. That's why I was so sure the assailant was a woman."

"That is a problem, I admit. Perhaps Dorothy Hedge wielded the bat. A warrant would still be a good idea."

"Are you sure Mama doesn't suspect you spotted it?"

"Absolutely. We are meeting tomorrow with a group of sympathetic students to fight against the Brady bill and encourage the government to do away with welfare as we know it, which seems to mean no more food stamps. I can hardly wait. Mama is very pleased to have an ally of her own sex and age; older women have sadly disappointed her on the whole."

Harriet moved toward the door, which Reed opened for her. "I'll tell Kate as soon as she returns or calls in," he said. "You really are quite wonderful, Harriet, in your own particular way." He kissed her cheek

213

and promised to see about the warrant as soon as possible.

"If possible, before I have to go and take part in a public protest against welfare," Harriet urged as she stepped into the elevator.

Kate, meanwhile, was on her way upstate, having had to wait on a line to pay cash since she did not possess an E-ZPass; she had purchased a token for her return trip, but fervently hoped that she would not again need to pass this way. She had spent her morning in endless conversations with members of the American Kennel Association, sounding to her own ears like a nutcase, but apparently she was a usual enough questioner to dog breeders. Her object had been to locate Marjorie, whose last name she did not know, let alone her address. Her first thought had been to ask Dorothy Hedge, pretending innocence about Hedge's true allegiances, but Hedge would no doubt have warned Marjorie. Even if Hedge did not warn Marjorie, she would herself begin to worry about Kate's intentions, clearly a result to be avoided.

And so Kate had got hold of a list of dog breeders in the area from the AKA—this alone had taken time—and had then called those in upstate New York, asking for the name of a woman who bred Saint Bernards. Eventually she had narrowed down her inquiries to two possibilities, one of whom turned out to be abandoning the breed and thus hadn't had a litter in several years. The other was Marjorie's Kennels, toward

214

which Kate was now heading, having, however, given Marjorie no warning of her imminent arrival. True, some eager AKA type might tell Marjorie someone had been inquiring about a Saint Bernard breeder, but surely there were legitimate enough inquiries of this sort. Kate, of course, planned simply, upon emerging from her car, to say that she had been overcome with a need to see Banny. After that, well, Kate had left without telling Reed where she was going because he would have asked what she intended to accomplish and in fact she hadn't a clue.

It did occur to her for one moment that she might be in danger, but Kate comforted herself with the fact that if someone, whoever that someone was, had wanted to kill her instead of kidnapping Reed, they could easily have done so already. Having reassured herself as she drove along the Taconic Parkway with such spurious arguments as these, she was feeling quite composed when she swung the car into Marjorie's driveway.

Kate had, of course, expected to be accosted by Marjorie and asked sharply who she was and what she wanted. But by the time she reached the end of a rather long driveway, Kate had spotted only some kennels and a young woman who was cleaning them out. The young woman, being hailed, told Kate that the owner of the kennels could be found in the house, pointing toward it in a rather vague way.

Kate parked the car in an area marked PARKING and

215

began to walk toward the house. But before she had gone far she looked up to find herself facing a woman with a gun, a rather long gun bent in the middle, as Kate put it to herself; she knew next to nothing about guns, but had the impression that handguns were most dangerous, and that everyone who lived in the country kept a shotgun about the place for protection. Kate had, in fact, picked up this piece of information, if it was information, from country neighbors in her childhood who lived in the country all year-round, and who used to tell Kate that their houses were never robbed because everyone knew that the owners kept guns.

The woman with the gun stood there, waiting for Kate to come closer. It did not for a moment occur to Kate that the woman might shoot her. The idea never even crossed her mind, as she later assured Reed. When the two women were a few feet apart, Kate stared for a moment and said: "Muriel."

"My name is Marjorie now, Kate Fansler." And the woman straightened the gun, snapping its parts together, and then held it facing down. "Come for Banny? Judith"—the woman called out to the young woman still cleaning the kennels—"bring Banny, will you?"

They stood there, like figures who, having been posed, were waiting to be photographed, until Judith returned with what was clearly, to Kate's amazement, a large, loping Saint Bernard, who rushed up to Kate, then over to Marjorie, then back to Kate. I couldn't possibly lift her now, Kate thought. She crouched on the ground and put her arms around the dog, who licked her face. Then Kate stood up.

"So the dog was part of the plot too," she said.

"Of course."

Kate looked at the woman, who if not recognizable as Muriel—for Kate could hardly recognize someone met only once after almost thirty years—still clearly *was* Muriel, though Kate hardly knew the reason for her certainty. Keeping them both in view, Banny lay down between the women as they stood there.

"So you've hated me all these years," Kate said, when it was clear no invitation to enter the house would be forthcoming. "I was twenty-two, Muriel— Marjorie—and behaved like a fool, I admit it. It wasn't my business to think up plots for my brother. He should have been left to manage his own life. But I would like to point out that you didn't have to reject him the moment he seemed not so rich. You could have waited and watched, you know."

"No, I don't know. You've always been rich. You never saw my mother working night and day, worn out, or my father proud of his honest poverty. Honest poverty! He drank after work, and her work never stopped. I wasn't going to live that life."

"What did it take to stay angry for nearly three decades?"

"You exaggerate your influence. I hardly thought of you until recently. But you lurked in the back of my mind. And the hatred I felt three decades ago returned to me full blast. When I hate, I discovered, I hate forever."

It occurred to Kate to say that they would not now be facing each other in this preposterous way if when Marjorie had loved she had loved forever. But Kate was beginning to realize that the woman facing her was hardly in a reasonable frame of mind. The barely concealed rage was making itself evident. Besides, Muriel's love for William had hardly been comparable to this moment's hatred.

"Marjorie," Kate said, taking a step forward. Banny raised her head. "Could we sit down and talk about this, perhaps have some tea? I know what I did then was wrong. I can even understand your passion for revenge, and the form it took—kidnapping Reed, I mean, and the rest of it. But how could you have murdered Toni, or attacked her so that she died of injuries to her brain?"

"I didn't attack her," Marjorie said. "You're still a fool. Well, I'm not a fool. I've no desire to spend the rest of my life in prison for murder, either of Toni or of you." And she slightly shifted the gun.

"Then who?" Kate began. But was there any point in asking? At least she was not to be shot, or not at any rate murdered. It came over Kate with dreadful conviction that Marjorie/Muriel was indeed mad, in the sense of insane. Would the promise of not murdering Kate allow Kate to turn her back, get into her
218

car, and depart? Somehow, Kate doubted it but was nonetheless near to deciding to try it.

"Toni was a fool," Marjorie said. "She didn't stick to the rules, or to her promises, or to the job she had undertaken."

"She worked for you?" Kate asked. Understanding was dawning upon Kate, slowly but surely. She had already figured out—this was largely why she had come to see Marjorie—that Toni had been a double agent. But Kate had assumed that Mama and perhaps Dorothy Hedge had hired her. Had Harriet known or suspected? Kate dismissed that fleeting question. "She worked for you?" Kate asked again.

"For me and the others. We were working to restore sanity to our country and to your university. Only when I realized that you worked at the university did the chance to avenge myself on you dawn upon me. I'm not very quick, which as you so rightly pointed out was evidenced by my not hanging around after your dirty trick years ago and working to mollify your brother."

"You are an admirer of Pat Buchanan and Pat Robertson?" Kate asked, hoping to swing the conversation to a political shouting match which might attract someone's attention—Judith's, or perhaps that of someone else about the place, another visitor or prospective purchaser viewing the kennels.

"Of course I admire them, and all the others you liberal bleeding hearts despise. We've let so-called

219

kindness eat away at this country's guts. It's disgusting what's taught in college these days, and I hear that you're one of the worst offenders with this feminist, multiracial shit. That was how your name came up. I must say when I heard it, it was like a revelation, like a religious conversion with light everywhere. I persuaded them to change their tactics a little. They didn't care. You were as good a target as any—and you were too proud to take your husband's name. Typical. If you had, I'd never have realized who you were. I only saw William one other time, and you weren't married then. Hearing the name Kate Fansler, I nearly peed in my pants with delight."

A thousand questions flooded Kate's mind, and like the little Dutch boy, he of the finger in the dike, she struggled to keep back the deluge. Getting out of here seemed the wisdom of the moment. Kate took a step away from Marjorie, but Marjorie waved her back.

"Sit, Banny," Marjorie said. The dog stood and then dropped its rear end to a sitting position. Banny looked at Marjorie for further orders, or some indication of what was happening. Marjorie raised her gun, did something Kate could hear to ready it, and pointed it at the sitting dog. Kate gasped, horror flooding in upon her.

Marjorie turned her eyes from the dog to Kate, but as the dog started to lie down again, Marjorie said: "Sit, Banny." Banny sat up. "No," Marjorie went on, "I wouldn't murder you and rot in jail. My other little plot didn't exactly work out, did it? Dorothy tells me you're fond of this creature. Good. Then watch me blow her to bits with this shotgun. And don't move. I don't really mind if I have to shoot you in the leg, although shotguns are notoriously inexact. You need rifles for that."

Marjorie knelt, the better to steady the gun, and took careful aim, and at that moment Kate raced across the space between them and threw herself on Marjorie. The gun went off, clearly missing Banny, whose bark could be heard. Kate tried to wrench the gun from the other woman, whose grip was amazingly powerful. Kate was taller, and had had surprise on her side, but now Marjorie began to fight, tossing aside the gun and throwing her weight onto Kate; she was by far the stronger, and Kate, despite her struggles, was soon pinned to the ground. Kate tried to push against the other woman, but seemed unable even to move her own limbs. Marjorie's hands went around Kate's neck and Kate felt the hands tighten. Struggling seemed only to increase the pressure of the other woman's grip.

"Marjorie?" Kate heard the voice of the kennel girl—or was it someone else? She heard Banny barking, and then she heard nothing at all.

Sometime later, when consciousness returned to Kate, she took up the struggle once again, thrashing about. She was still being held down.

"Kate, Kate, stop fighting. It's me; it's Reed. You're in the hospital. You're all right, Kate."

"Banny?"

"Banny's all right too. Everyone's all right. But my God, you might have been killed. Do you never stop to think of the trouble you are to me? Does it never occur to you to tell a person where you're going? I've had a ghastly time."

" ' "I weep for you," the Walrus said: "I deeply sympathise." ' " Kate managed a smile, but even that small motion, and her speaking, made her throat ache and she winced.

"You've also got a black eye and a nasty head wound. I hope you're satisfied. And don't quote anything else to me. Just rest. Let me do the talking, if any."

"Did you save me?" Kate whispered.

"I only wish. No, my dear, you were saved by a wonderful young woman named Judith who works for Marjorie and apparently took the scene in without standing around asking questions, as would no doubt have been your response. As far as I can gather, she picked up the shotgun by the muzzle end and swung it for all she was worth. It caught Marjorie in the head, and she's got a beauty of a concussion. It seems the kennel girl plays golf in her spare time."

"Marj—" Kate croaked.

"Try not to talk. I know that's like asking a seal not to swim, but make an effort. Having taken a golf swing, the promptly acting Judith called an ambulance and here the two of you are, in the same small town hospital but in widely separated rooms. You will be asked, upon recovery, if you want to press charges. Marjorie, of course, may decide to accuse you of assault and attempted robbery of a Saint Bernard, but fortunately we have a witness in dear, never-to-be-sufficiently-appreciated Judith. Who is, by the way, staying on to tend to the dogs until Marjorie regains her health."

"Not dies like Toni?"

"No. No fear. It wasn't, oddly enough, nearly that serious a blow. It all depends, apparently, on where you hit someone and with what strength. Toni was smashed more directly and harder than Marjorie. Our golf champion succeeded in getting her off you, but not in seriously endangering her life. I gather she didn't even knock her out."

"Sorry."

"I should jolly well think so. Now, listen. Leslie and Harriet are outside and want to see you and say a brief hello. They will be allowed in only if you promise not to move or utter a word. Agreed? And don't shake your head, you fool, that only makes the pain worse. Raise one finger for yes, two fingers for no."

Kate raised a finger and Reed opened the door to two very anxious women.

"You look like hell," Harriet said. "I thought I was the one who was being a private eye. Don't answer, you're not supposed to talk."

"I'm glad they kidnapped Reed and not you," Leslie said. "You'd probably have forced them to kill you in the first hour you were with them. Imagine your getting into a knock-down, drag-out fight. And one thinks one knows one's dearest friends!"

Sixteen

A week later Reed drove Kate home from the hospital. Kate still had the feeling that her neck didn't turn quite as it ought to and that a headache might start at any moment, but she was planning to return to teaching, having missed only a few classes.

After leaving the hospital they had stopped off at Marjorie's kennels. Marjorie was not there, or if there, had chosen not to appear. But Judith was, and greeted them pleasantly. After waving from alongside the kennels, she had emerged with Banny beside her. Banny was not yet as large as she would become, but she was a big dog now, with a big dog's dignity. Since she was also a Saint Bernard, she walked unhurriedly, with what one might in another connection have called measured steps, her great tail waving slowly like a plume.

"Want to get in, Banny?" Reed had said, holding open the back door of the car. Banny, seeming to have grasped without major effort both that these two were now her people, and that she was too big a dog to ride with them in front, settled herself on the backseat, her tail still waving gently.

"Goodbye, Banny my love," Judith called. "You come see me when you're a mama, hear?"

Kate turned her neck so sharply toward Reed as he backed up the car that she winced, whether at the pain or at the thought of Banny's motherhood was hard even for her to distinguish.

"Anything more you didn't tell me?" Kate asked. "We're going to have puppies?"

"Not immediately. The negotiations were a bit complicated, and seemed, apart from the astronomical price, to rest on an agreement to let Banny breed. It seems she's a rare specimen who, mated with another rare specimen, is a natural to bring forth future champions. I had to agree. We can't keep any of the puppies, which I had to agree to if her price was to be lowered into a sphere of financial sanity, but I didn't think you'd want them anyway. As to Banny, I was told on good authority that a mother dog can't wait to see the end of puppies once they're weaned and wouldn't know them if they came up to her with their pedigrees around their necks. Banny will now feel like a regretful woman who had to give her baby up for adoption. So that seemed acceptable."

Kate was aware of an enormous tiredness, not fatigue exactly, which one felt after great exertions, but the tiredness of too much worry and of not having had sufficient rest for too long a time. "I suppose you've settled all sorts of matters without me," she said with a petulance she knew to be entirely unjustified. She couldn't seem to prevent herself from complaint. Reed said it was the aftershock, and not to worry.

"You wanted Banny," he said. "So did I. All the time in the hospital, you kept talking about Banny."

"Well, that damn woman nearly shot her. In cold blood. And now she seems to be demanding as much money for her as if she hadn't tried to kill the poor beast in front of my eyes."

"It's complicated," Reed said. "Judith is managing the kennels for her, and being very businesslike as is only proper. Banny is a valuable dog."

"Bitch—I know that much. Are you valuable, Banny?" Kate said, reaching a hand back without quite turning her head. Banny's plume waved in confirmation. "Have you thought how we're going to manage?" Kate asked Reed. "We both work all day on many days, just for starters."

"You'd be amazed, Kate, to know the canine services available. Dog walkers, all sorts of people in the dog business. We'll manage."

"Any other news you're planning to break to me

before we get home? I'd appreciate some warning if you've undertaken other profound renovations in our life."

"Oh, come off it, Kate. Not that I begrudge you the exquisite pleasure of having Banny forced upon you when you want her but hardly dare to say so. After all, you saved her life, you've a right to grumble."

"Do you think we should go on calling her Banny? Any name given by that dotty woman may carry bad vibes."

"There's nothing wrong with Anne Bancroft, is there? It's not as though the dog had been named Marilyn Monroe or Joan Crawford. Obviously one couldn't put up with that."

"I see your point."

"Good. The only other news is that Harriet will be there as a welcoming committee, and Archie as well, to explain the legal ins and outs. He's been attending to what we might call The Case while I've been attending to you. But if you're too tired, we can call it off."

"It sounds just the distraction I require. Did they get a lot of information out of Marjorie?"

"Some. Now stop talking, close your eyes, and think only about long walks with Banny until we get home."

"Long walks?"

"You've got to get into shape, Kate. Get your muscles into shape, I mean. You're out of practice, and that woman could have killed you. Didn't you ever fight with anyone? Never wrestled with your brothers and learned something about self-defense? I can't think what the use is in having three brothers if they didn't teach you how to fight."

"They were too much older to fight with me. I wasn't worth the effort. I don't think they really taught me anything, except how frightfully dull and pompous men could be. Having learned that, I searched for their opposite and found you."

"I don't know if that's a compliment, and I do know that it's in no way true, but thank you all the same. As to the walks, I'll do the mornings, you do the evenings, and one of us, or someone else, will function in between. You'll discover a whole new meaning to life."

"I had enough meaning before all this happened, Reed. Although perhaps I didn't know how much I would care if someone snatched you away. And I didn't know that having had Banny for a while, I could not possibly let her out of my life. But none of this is to deny how perfectly happy I was before this whole sorry episode started."

"Close your eyes and try to relax," Reed said.

"E. M. Forster noticed that everyone in America is always telling everyone else to relax. But I'll try."

When the four of them had, as Reed had warned, settled down for an extended consultation in the living room, Kate was lying on the couch under a light blanket with a pillow at her head. "I feel exactly like Elizabeth Barrett-not-yet-Browning," Kate said, "though Banny is nothing like Flush." Banny was lying beside the couch and Kate's hand rested, from time to time, on the dog's large head, causing the tail to wave gently in response. Harriet, Archie, and Reed sat in chairs grouped around the couch. "We look like one of those Victorian paintings of a domestic scene," Archie observed.

"Entitled *The Reckoning*, no doubt," Reed added. "You begin, Kate, offering if you possibly can a brief but coherent account of why you rushed off to confront Marjorie in that ill-considered way."

"I suggest we omit personal attacks from this discussion," Kate said, removing her hand from Banny's head; Banny sighed deeply. "But I do admit, since you put it so delicately, that my actions were probably not the wisest. It was like this. After talking to Harriet about the ad for Banny and one thing and another, I began to realize that Toni must have been working for the other side, at least at the beginning. That seemed to explain why she had hired Harriet as a means of getting to me. Not," Kate added with emphasis, "that Harriet didn't turn out to be a damn good private eye. I'm certain Toni would have continued with her as partner if assault, attempted murder, and eventual murder had not intervened. Could I have some water?"

Reed went to fetch a pitcher of water, returning with glasses and a bottle of single malt Scotch. "I thought we might need some fortification," he explained, pouring the water for Kate.

"I'm actually thirsty for water," Kate announced, quaffing a large amount of the stuff. "I shall lie here in clarity and purity, while you three imbibe. Liquor isn't supposed to mix with whatever it is I'm taking, and to tell you the truth, strange as it seems, I don't want any of the hard stuff. I am certain it would give me a blinding headache. Now, how's that for the effects of being throttled?" And she touched her neck.

"To continue, then, without the aid of alcohol, I reasoned thus: the only person who could possibly have been Muriel was Marjorie, and the more I thought about it the likelier it seemed. She had hired Toni to work out the plot, probably telling her some wild tale or other, and Toni had arranged the kidnapping and all that followed with the aid of Bad Boy and his mother. I set off to confront Marjorie or Muriel, really with the idea of suggesting that this grudge had got a little out of hand, and maybe we could talk the matter out. Don't interrupt," she added, as both Reed and Harriet seemed about to burst into anguished speech. "I know it wasn't the world's brightest idea, but you asked what I was doing and I'm telling you." She took some more water, and Reed refilled her glass.

"While I was exchanging remarks with Marjorie, however, she standing there with that gun and Banny between us"—here her hand descended again onto the dog's head—"she said something about recognizing my name when she heard it and joining in the

231

fun and games. Well, something like that. So I guessed that she hadn't been the one to initiate the plot but had joined in later. I was about to wave a flag of truce, when she announced that she was going to shoot Banny. You all know what happened then.

"So what have I figured out since? I know"—she motioned to Reed with her other hand—"I was only supposed to tell you what I was doing, but surely my conclusions are part of what I was doing. Anyway, I'm going to tell you. It won't take long, and will take even less time if you stop interrupting me."

Reed threw back the Scotch in one dramatic gulp, as they do in Western movies, and adopted an expression of determined silence.

"That's better," Kate said. "There's not much more, really. I've more or less decided that Mama and the right-wing types were behind the kidnapping scheme before Marjorie got wind of it—probably from Dorothy Hedge, whom, after all, she knew—and decided to join in the fun. Over to you all," she said. Harriet and Reed looked at Archie.

"It's odd as it's worked out," Archie said. "When Reed brought me into this rather odd situation, he explained that you had at first thought it was a right-wing plot, and then had decided, upon the advice of Emma Wentworth—whom, by the way, I know and respect—that an individual was behind it. Emma was wrong about its being a colleague, but she at least got you to consider an angry individual as the instigator. Thus you first suspected Kate's less enlightened colleagues, and then, at the suggestion of Kate's friend Leslie—and it was a damn smart suggestion—you began to search for a revengeful individual from Kate's past, someone Kate might have forgotten but who had certainly not forgotten her. The intriguing fact, at least from my point of view as an outsider who was persuaded into looking at the situation"—here he glared at Reed—"by the high-handed calling in of a good many chips, is that all the suppositions were in part correct." He paused to sip his Scotch, eschewing Reed's dramatics.

"Like Kate, but for different reasons, I determined that Muriel, if she existed, and unless she had some close connection to the university, could hardly have instigated the whole thing. I didn't then know, of course, that she had joined the Kate Fansler offensive at a later date. The question for me became, how did all this begin?

"I had one advantage over the rest of you. I knew none of the players and could therefore begin to examine the situation with an open mind. I had been called in to defend Harriet from charges, should any be made, but the police had no grounds on which to hold her and only interviewed her. All of you demonstrated great faith in Harriet's innocence of the plot and of the attack on Toni, but to me at first she seemed the likeliest suspect. I've already explained this to Harriet," he added, glancing her way. Harriet raised her glass to him in a mocking salute.

"Several things ultimately convinced me that she

233

was innocent," he continued. "First, I did a certain amount of checking back through her history with Toni, and it seemed clear enough that she had not joined Toni's outfit in order to undertake this siege against Kate. By then I had decided that the woman Harriet had met in the ladies' room was probably Toni's attacker. And I then did what, if you three will forgive me, you ought to have thought of a lot sooner. I do realize that clear thinking was hardly to be expected under the circumstances in which you all found yourselves, but I have to brag a little to justify imbibing this excellent booze."

"What did we overlook?" Kate asked. "Break it to me gently."

"I got hold of the university's record of suits against them by women who failed to get tenure. My aim was to find someone with a special grudge against Kate. No," he said, in answer to Kate's smacking herself on the forehead in self-rebuke, and then wincing from the pain, "in whatever flattering light I am succeeding in putting myself, do remember that Reed had been kidnapped, Kate had been threatened with the possibility of having to publicly refute her deepest convictions about feminism, and Reed, when rescued, admitted to having been sexually tempted by nymphets. None of these are situations likely to clear the mind. But to continue:

"It didn't take very much time to go through the tenure fights, particularly since the records I was examining were of women who had sued, gone to court.

The great number of women unfairly denied tenure do not sue, and were not, therefore, in the proceedings I was examining. I hoped, naturally enough, for a suit against the English department, which would obviously have involved Kate, but there wasn't one. Nor, though I'd hoped, had I expected it, since the likelihood of Kate's not remembering a suit in her own department was remote. Sorry, I seem to be being rather long-winded about this—a habit of the profession when addressing a jury, arising from the need to cover all the necessary details.

"Well, I found the tenure case, and what was more, Kate had been involved in it, though only at a very late stage. A standing committee of tenured faculty had been appointed to evaluate all disputed tenure reviews, and someone not in the department of the suer was assigned to head the committee and write the final report. It will hardly astonish you to learn that Kate was, in this case, the head of the committee. The woman suing was in the physical education department and it was one of those difficult and disturbing cases."

"Can I have simply forgotten the whole thing? There were so many threats of suits some years ago," Kate said. "Often, however, those who seemed to have the best cases didn't choose to sue. I think I had some responsibility for that. I'd known women who sued universities back in the Seventies, and I was well aware of the personal price they paid, in their health, their relationships, their sanity. I was often

235

asked my personal opinion, and always emphasized the price of suing, as well as the university's habit of fighting such cases with no holds barred. Nothing in the woman's past life would be out of bounds to them. To be fair, this is probably true of all universities, but I only knew mine and the few cases I had heard of elsewhere."

"Exactly," Archie said in consoling tones. "This case was not atypical. The one woman whom no one liked or could support, neither her own department nor her students, nonetheless insisted on going through with it. This particular woman in the physical education department put a great strain on all the tenured women who would have come to the aid of someone they respected, or for whom there was even any genuine support. In the end, Kate wrote a report explaining the inability of any members of the Association of Tenured Women to support the woman in this suit. Her name, of course, was, or became, Dorothy Hedge. She waited for revenge, planning it, hiring Toni, using her mother's and brother's right-wing connections, and she didn't have to wait as long as Muriel. Barely six years, in fact."

"I'm going to slit my throat," Kate said. "Quietly, making no mess, but with a firm hand. My God, it's as though my whole life has paraded before me as a dismal failure. Don't try to console me," she said, as the others began murmuring comforting sounds. "I seem to have been a wonderful feminist, no doubt about that. At least two women wanted to kill me, or

236

destroy me, endangering my husband while they were at it. It hardly seems the crown on a career of successful feminism or even humanity. No," she added, as Reed offered her a drink, hoping it might calm her down. "I am simply going to die or to become a fugitive like Lord Jim, lurking about in hot climates. I hate hot climates. Oh, God!" It was a cry worthy of someone with faith actually calling upon an exalted deity.

Reed got to his feet but was pushed down again by Harriet, who also glared Archie into silence.

"Now you listen to me, Kate Fansler! I don't want to hear another word of this shit. Because that's what it is: shit. Emerson said a person who made no enemies never made anything else, and someone else said you knew who a person was by knowing who her or his enemies were. Sure, you pissed off two women, and I have to say that you certainly did a good job of it, they stayed good and pissed from that day to this. Do you want me to hold a celebration in Radio City Music Hall and invite all the women you've encouraged, assisted, persuaded, swayed into good actions and brave deeds? Because it will be a lot more than two, you can bet on that. Don't interrupt!

"It occurs to me that if anyone were going to indulge in an orgy of self-immolation, it should be me. *I.* I let Toni flatter me into working with her; then, when she seems to have decided to change sides, or whatever she decided, she continued to manipulate me with exquisite skill, I who am supposed to have

237

the savoir faire of Anthony Blunt and the chutzpah of Kim Philby. And while you're berating yourself with failure properly to serve womankind, my dear Kate, let me point out that you stuck by me when you had a damn good reason to think I'd knocked Toni off. So shut the fuck up, and stop feeling so mea culpa, not to say sorry for yourself. Have I made my views sufficiently clear? I can go on."

And tossing her remaining Scotch down her throat in imitation of Reed, she sat down, still glaring at Kate.

"I couldn't have put it better myself," Reed said. "I would only point out that women attacking women is the hottest game in town, particularly feminist turncoats who want a lot more attention than they've been getting, not to mention book sales. There are two infallible signs of a revolution's success: a vigorous backlash and turncoats. You, my dear, have become the chosen object of both. It's a compliment, in a way."

"I'll try not to become narcissistic and self-pitying," Kate said. "I think I will venture upon a drink after all. The headache, if any, will be mine, and so will the relief from having to watch you all tossing the stuff back as though it were rotgut."

Reed handed her a glass, and she sipped at it. "You look white as a sheet," Archie said. "Perhaps we'd better go."

"Sheets are now brightly colored, with designer patterns," Kate said. "I shall resemble one of them shortly, if I can't clear up a few points. I gather that
238

Marjorie heard about the whole caper from Dorothy and, recognizing my name, joined in. That, doubtless, is how Toni got her name and persuaded her to put in the ad you saw." This was directed at Harriet.

"Probably," Harriet said. "But Toni had used a dog and Ovido—he of the vet's and dog training place—for messages before. It's a pretty clever dodge. And I would like to point out, Kate, while you're blaming yourself for the failures of your womanhood, that if you hadn't stopped letting Toni run the show and gotten over your unaccustomed passivity, the whole plot might have worked a lot better. I think it was when I flushed out those girls in that university apartment that Toni began to change her mind about whom she wanted to work for. But that's just a guess."

"So it was Dorothy Hedge who hit Toni with her brother's baseball bat. Or was it Bad Boy himself?"

"We may never know," Archie said. "But I'm pretty sure it was the Hedge woman."

"I agree," Harriet said. "You have to remember that Dorothy Hedge had years of resentment bottled up. When Toni deserted her for the other side, she must have felt very last strawish—murderous, in fact. I think that's how it must have been."

"I'm also pretty sure she was the one in the ladies' room with Harriet," Archie said. "Once Harriet has identified her, we'll know for sure. One of the problems with this situation from the beginning has been that so many of the players didn't meet. Harriet never met Hedge, and Kate met Marjorie rather late in the game."

"I owe you many thanks, heartfelt I assure you," Kate said to Archie. "You didn't in the end have to defend Harriet, but you certainly kept your head better than the rest of us—well, certainly better than I did."

Kate looked across at Harriet. Having shot off her mouth about her own feelings of guilt and regret, feelings she knew would never really dissolve or cease to trouble her, she now turned her attention to Harriet, who had been duped into a job and used in a plot against her friends. "I hope," she said to Harriet, "you haven't decided to desert the detective business. You may not, heaven be praised, offer either Sam Spade or Philip Marlowe serious competition, but I think you have a flair for the business. And I haven't a doubt, by the way, that it was you and your presence throughout this miserable business that turned poor Toni around."

"Not to worry," Harriet said. "I'm still in the private eye game, and I've got a new partner. As young as Toni, but male this time. We met in the course of another case preceding yours, and he thought the idea of using an old dame like me was the bee's knees. He wants to start his own firm, and while I didn't like to abandon Toni, who had, or so I thought, treated me most kindly, I got back in touch with him when Archie had figured all this out. I asked him if the offer was still open. I told him all about how I had been used, of course, but also about how clever I had been. So we're in business. Let me give you each a card, in the fervent hope that you wouldn't require t, except for Archie, of course. Archie has promised to send some business our way."

Kate looked at Harriet with admiration. Everyone except Kate stood, the meeting having concluded itself. Banny too arose.

"I think she wants to go out," Reed said.

"So do I," Kate said. "No, don't argue with me. Banny and I will take a short stroll together in the park."

"Don't forget to take a Baggie and a leash," Harriet said.

"I'll take the Baggie, but not the leash. Banny will stick by me, won't you Banny?" Kate said.

"Take the leash just to have one," Harriet said, handing Kate an elegant leather leash and a collar. Attached to the collar was a tag (BANNY FANSLER/ AMHEARST) with the address and the telephone number. "From me and Archie," Harriet said.

"You two have everything figured out, don't you?" Kate said. "Come on, Banny." And having fastened the collar around Banny's neck, Kate departed with the dog.

There was a momentary silence.

"She's taking it hard," Harriet said.

"Yes," Reed said. "I'm afraid she sees it as a total failure on her part from beginning to end. She might have figured it out for herself, you know, given time and freedom from throttling. We'll never know."

"Cheer up," Harriet said. "After all, the same dreadful people are still out there, with grudges against people like Kate. We mustn't give up now."

"Who's giving up?" Reed said, as they moved toward the door. "By the way, I have some news. Banny is to be allowed a dalliance with a prize Saint Bernard, but only if she likes him, of course. Stay tuned."

From the living room window, when the others had departed, Reed watched Kate and Banny enter the park. He could only guess at Kate's feelings, although his was certainly an educated guess. Banny's feelings, however, were simple and evident as she ambled along beside Kate, the plume tail swaying.

From the master of the American literary mystery
come these short stories—
including eight mysteries featuring Kate Fansler:

* * *

AMANDA CROSS

THE
COLLECTED STORIES

* * *

A *People* "Page-Turner of the Week"

"For more than twenty-five years,
Amanda Cross has been blazing a trail for the rest
to follow."—SARA PARETSKY

Available in trade paperback from Ballantine Books.

A TRADITION OF QUALITY

AMANDA CROSS

The Kate Fansler Mysteries

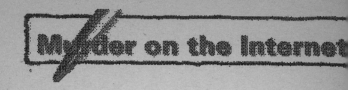